NO FOOTBALLS IN THE PLAYGROUND

All the very best,
Andrew Slater

Andrew J. Slater

Andrew Slater taught for many years, working in both primary and secondary schools. These days he is a Senior Lecturer in Teaching Studies at the College of Ripon and York St John.

Andrew J Slater asserts the moral right to be identified as the author of this book.

All the characters in this publication are entirely fictitious.

Drawings by Natasha, Ben and Charlie Slater

Published by Leyburn Clovelly

© Andrew J. Slater 2001

ISBN 0 954028 80 5

Printed by York Publishing Services Ltd,
64 Hallfield Road, Layerthorpe, York Y031 7ZQ

TO ANGIE

**with thanks for
Natasha, Ben and Charlie**

It is realities, not appearances, which count.

CONTENTS

One	Don't forget the new boy	1
Two	Please get me to my class	4
Three	Balraj meets some bullies	7
Four	Balraj makes a friend	12
Five	Bad news	15
Six	Not fair	20
Seven	Are we ready?	26
Eight	Mavis and the box	31
Nine	A cold, damp Friday	35
Ten	Watch that foot	41
Eleven	The Cupboards Inspector	45
Twelve	Is Ms Granger angry?	52
Thirteen	Look before you leg-it	57
Fourteen	Inspectors have their say	63
Fifteen	Now the week is over	68
Sixteen	The Big Match	71

SOME CHARACTERS

Hoddle Street Juniors: Pupils
Balraj Singh
Marcus Linton Beckford
Bernard Finlay
Charmaine Bradley
The Lewis Twins
Tim Tomkinson
Belinda Pollard

Hoddle Street Juniors: Staff
Alan Ramsbottom – Deputy Headteacher
Ms Granger – Headteacher
Mrs Hussain – Head of Lower School
Mr Johnstone – Head of Upper School
Tom – Schoolkeeper
Maureen Witherspoon – Teacher
Mrs Khan – Teaching Assistant
Leroy Jones – Teacher
Sally Green – Secretary
Linda Cooper – New teacher

Others
Mrs Piper – Chief ROFTOT Inspector
Hector Potts
Millicent Bourne Cosin
Jed Langley – Football Coach from Bridley Town FC
And ... the short, bearded, heavily after-shaved Inspector

Relatives
Hardeep Singh – Balraj's cousin
Gary Ramsbottom – Professional Footballer, Alan's Son
Mavis Ramsbottom – Alan's Wife

ONE: DON'T FORGET THE NEW BOY

'The new boy's folder is waiting on your desk,' announced the fox-faced Headteacher, Ms Granger, from the staffroom door. She fixed her sights on a middle-aged man who was standing by the kettle holding a giant mug. 'Collect him when the bell goes and try to remember to test his reading before you take him down to Mrs Witherspoon.'

Alan Ramsbottom gulped a mouthful of tea, took his jacket from the back of a chair and hurried to his office. Knowing that the room would be locked, he didn't try the door. Instead, he placed his jacket on the corridor carpet and began to search for his keys. Inside his top pocket his fingers came into contact with a glue-like substance. Groaning inwardly, he realised that this had once been a chocolate.

It was at moments like this that Alan half regretted that the children down in Year 3 were so generous. Hoddle Street was a most friendly school, but a stream of coughs and colds had convinced him that it was best only to eat wrapped sweets. The pockets of his ageing jacket often bulged with chocolates which had passed through numerous hands before finding their final resting place.

Alan found his chocolate-coated keys. He took out his handkerchief, wiped the keys, opened the door and, passing beneath the sign marked 'Deputy', went inside. His eyes moved to the thick folder waiting on his desk, but he was disturbed by a loud yell from the playground outside. He hurried to the window, almost dislodging a flower pot from its perch on top of his bookcase in the process. Using his shirt sleeve, he wiped the coating of condensation off the window and peered outside.

NO FOOTBALLS IN THE PLAYGROUND

In the middle of the playground stood Robin Johnstone, tall and still as the Statue of Liberty. With arm outstretched, he held an orange football up above his head. Around his knees a crowd of sheepish boys from Year 4 was gathering.

For a moment, Alan was puzzled. Two teachers were always on playground duty during morning break. Where, then, was Miss Cooper? On Mondays Hoddle Street's youngest teacher was often to be seen clutching her coffee cup and standing like an angry military policeman in the middle of the older boys' favourite football pitch.

It took little time to work out what was happening. Out of the corner of his eye, the Deputy watched as Miss Cooper marched someone off the playground at a yomping good pace. Mildly irritated, he continued to watch until she passed behind the line of shrubs which shielded the side entrance to the school building. He sighed, and like a demolition expert waiting for an explosion, started to count: 10,9,8,7,6,5,4,3,2 …

The peace of the corridor was suddenly shattered. Without even pausing to knock, Miss Cooper burst straight into the office. 'Look at me,' she wailed. 'My trousers are ruined. This boy's just spilt my coffee. He says he's new to the school, but that's no excuse, is it? Ms Granger should send him straight back to the school he has come from.'

The Deputy looked at Miss Cooper and then at the apparently crestfallen boy by her side. He wasn't quite sure what to say. Was Miss Cooper making a fuss about an accident? Why didn't she move around as all the more experienced teachers did when out on the playground?

Miss Cooper continued to complain. It seemed, however, as if the Deputy was no longer listening. With the air of someone who had lost something important, he rummaged around in his pocket before speaking. After a moment or two, he pulled out a chalk-coated chocolate. The discovery seemed to loosen his under-used tongue. 'Look, Miss Cooper,' he whispered. 'I think we need to talk this over on our own.' He cleared his throat before using the extra deep voice developed for telling children off. *'Go outside, young man, whilst I speak to your teacher.'*

The high pitched tone of the internal phone interrupted before he could continue. Alan grabbed the receiver and, speaking in a gentle voice, several notes higher than his trusted 'pupil-blaster', said, 'Not now, Sally. I'm very busy.'

The Deputy turned once again to Miss Cooper, keen to offer well meant, friendly advice. A large coffee stain snaking its way from knee to ankle of her trousers caught his eye and he hesitated. His voice faltered for a moment before beginning a journey through even higher octaves as he searched for the right words. 'Now, Linda,' he said, after some delay, 'don't forget you're new to teaching. With children you have to learn to expect the unexpected, you know.'

He looked again at her trousers and hesitated once more. Unsure what to do or say, he scratched the back of his large bald head. Then, as if acting on a sudden impulse, he plunged his hand into his pocket and pulled out his handkerchief. He tried another special voice. This time the slow but very kind one which he usually kept for his own two toddling grandchildren. 'Look, I'm very sorry this happened. But I'm sure that when you've dabbed your trousers they won't look too bad. The lines of coffee just look like extra stalks on the flowers really.'

Miss Cooper's watery eyes moved to Alan's chocolate-coated handkerchief. Without a word she turned and rushed from the room.

The phone sounded again, interrupting the thoughts of the handkerchief–holding Deputy. It was the office once more. He picked up the receiver and heard the now urgent voice of Sally, the secretary. 'Look, Alan, your appointment says that he really must go in a moment. Are you coming over or not?'

The Deputy didn't even wait to reply. Forgetting that Balraj Singh, the small, patient and by now puzzled newcomer, was still waiting in the corridor, he charged out of his room.

TWO: PLEASE GET ME TO MY CLASS!

The distance between the new Administration Block and the main school building worried Alan Ramsbottom. Walking at a reasonable pace and keeping to the recently laid pathway it took over two minutes. But when, as now, there was a need for haste Alan reckoned on halving the time. By leaping over a low fence and cutting across the 'out of bounds' lawn he reached his destination in a little under a minute.

He need not have bothered. A quick glance into the waiting area outside the General Office confirmed his greatest fear: he was already too late. Jed Langley had gone. How foolish he had been to allow himself to be distracted by other jobs! Somehow he had managed to miss the all-important planning meeting to discuss the school football team's great day out.

Most upset at missing an appointment fixed for well over a fortnight, the Deputy turned into the office and slumped into the empty swivel chair by the 'phone. Would Jed still want to use Hoddle Street children on the day of the opening of Bridley Town's new all-seater stadium?

As if anxious to avoid eye contact, Sally kept her gaze fixed on her computer screen. Her fingers moved with the speed of a finalist in the Young Musician of the Year as she worked on the report of last night's meeting of the school governors.

'Couldn't you have done something to delay him? Offer him a cup of tea or some of those nice cakes from over in the canteen?' grumbled Alan, looking far from happy. 'Bridley Town are bound to drop us now. After all, it's no skin off their noses. They could just as easily choose Chariot Combined.'

Looking up from her screen, Sally considered how to put her smooth secretarial skills to best use. She smiled patiently as she listened to all Alan's gloomy fears. She wisely resisted the temptation to ask whether football clubs really could have noses. When eventually the Deputy was quiet, she manoeuvred her wheel chair between her desk and the filing cabinets which made her corner of the office so cramped. With a reassuring twinkle in her light grey eyes, she held up a note loosely attached to a bundle of promotional leaflets about Bridley Town's new football stadium. 'When you've had time to read this you'll find there's no problem. Jed just wants you to ring him at the end of afternoon school.'

A smile returned to brighten Alan's worried face. Muttering 'Thanks', he shot out of the General Office, clutching the leaflets tightly to his chest like a winner's medal. Moving with a surprising turn of pace, like an athlete in a veterans' race, he hurdled the fence surrounding the 'out of bounds' lawn and sped on into the library. There he stopped suddenly and dropped the leaflets onto a display cabinet crammed full of house trophies. The wise words of his G.P., Meg Lonsdale, flashed through his mind. 'Try to slow down and make sure that you always eat your lunch,' she had advised only last week. He felt his chest suspiciously. Confident that his heart was still pumping, he sprinted on his way.

Back in his own office, Alan sat down at his desk. The rhythmic ticking of the clock on the wall signalled that time was passing quickly. 11.30 already! Only half an hour left before lunch break and a spell 'on duty' in the canteen. Automatically, the Deputy reached beneath his desk and pulled out a large red flask and a battered plastic sandwich box. He poured himself a cup of strong brown tea and devoted his full attention to an inviting cheese and pickle roll.

Between bites he vaguely remembered that he had something important to do. He scanned the piles of papers on his desk hoping that something would trigger his memory, until his eyes settled on a file perched on top of his in-tray. Half out-loud he read the words on the cover:

Sweeton Combined School
Records
Singh Balraj

The Deputy scanned through the pages: old test scores, photocopies of old reports, one or two letters from home. This was a job he always enjoyed. Although absent-minded, Alan rarely forgot important information about new children. His attention was drawn to the most recent report from Year 5. According to a Miss Hufton, 'Balraj started to do quite well during the Spring Term'. The Deputy read on, pleased to see that the new pupil had also begun to 'make up for all that time wasted down in Year 4'. The unseen Miss Hufton noted something else which was well worth knowing. Apparently Balraj often seemed to grin at the wrong moment. What would Mrs Witherspoon make of that?

The thought of the fearsome Mrs Witherspoon caused a sudden panic. Where was Balraj? Shouldn't he have taken him to class already? Anxiously dropping his second cheese and pickle roll onto his desk, Alan leapt to his feet. The new boy hadn't been in the corridor outside his room a moment or two ago. Where could he be?

A firm knock on the door interrupted before panic could turn into action. Hurriedly hiding the half-eaten roll in the desk drawer and wiping breadcrumbs from his trousers, he opened the door. Mrs Green, the towering part-time Music teacher, stood outside next to a teetering pile of drums. Like an opera star on a third curtain call, Mrs Green sang into action. 'I was sorting out the Music Hut just in case ROFTOT inspectors arrive earlier than expected when I saw this boy grinning at the rabbits in the school garden. Is he supposed to be with you? Anyway, he's kindly volunteered to carry the new drums over to the Hut. I'll send him back in a couple of minutes. He's being very useful.'

Before the Deputy could reply, a faint voice sounded from somewhere beneath the drums.

'Please, sir. Can I go to class, sir? You just went, sir. But I tried to find you and I couldn't. And then I saw the rabbit hutches and went to look. And this lady got me. And I've been carrying drums ever since, sir. Please take me. I'll be good. Promise.'

THREE: BALRAJ MEETS SOME BULLIES

Always smartly turned out in outfits chosen from an endless supply of neatly pressed skirts and carefully ironed blouses, Mrs Maureen Witherspoon looked much the same as any other middle-sized primary teacher in early middle age.

Yet her appearance was misleading. Children new to 6Q discovered two of life's most important lessons in double quick time. They didn't need to turn to the pages of a well-worn detective story to learn that you may not be able to tell what someone is like just by looking at their clothes. Nor did they need a Citizenship lesson to learn that you can be bullied by someone you know well.

Ever since her now dimly distant first week at Hoddle Street, Mrs Witherspoon had gained a reputation for being moody and aggressive. It was perhaps because her moods seemed to change so often and not just because she could be so fierce that Mrs Witherspoon upset everyone so much. One day she could be as nice as apple pie and cream and the next as sharp as a viper's bite. Though still a little under forty, Mrs Witherspoon seemed to have taught at Hoddle Street for longer than anyone could remember. More and more nowadays it was obvious that most of the children and several of the younger teachers fresh from Banchester University were scared of her.

Mavis, Alan's wife, had a theory. 'I'm sure her bark is far worse than her bite,' she would say late in the evenings when the couple ate biscuits and sipped hot chocolate. Alan wasn't convinced. Over the years he had learnt a lot about Maureen Witherspoon. He knew, for example, that she disliked changes and that, most of all, she hated gaining extra boys in her class.

Hoddle Street Juniors had always been known for its

friendliness. On classroom doors brightly coloured notices in seven different languages greeted visitors:

Welcome !!!!!!!
Knock once and walk straight in.

Every day Alan popped into such rooms, eager to see how work was going. It was undoubtedly the best thing of all about his job.

But somehow Mrs Witherspoon's room was different. Indeed, in recent weeks an aggressive notice warning off would-be visitors had appeared on her door. Written in large, bold print its message was very direct:

Class 6Q always works to achieve targets
Visitors waste time
Go away!!!!!!

Had this been put up as a challenge to Ms Granger? Up to now the young Headteacher had done nothing about it, preferring, apparently, to turn a 'blind eye'. In the old days when Mrs 'Blaster' Bullcock was Headmistress no such nonsense would have been allowed. She would have marched straight to the classroom and pulled the notice down!

Outside the door Alan hesitated, seemingly reluctant to knock. Fumbling in his pocket, he found his spotted handkerchief and wiped cold sweat from his forehead. Could he pluck up courage? 'Can't I go into my class, sir?' asked Balraj. The boy's request seemed to make up Alan's mind, for the Deputy took two deep breaths and stepped forward more decisively. His firm knock triggered an immediate and equally loud response from Mrs Witherspoon. 'Go away. Can't you see I'm teaching.'

Alan tried again.

Again the reply was instantaneous.

'Clear off.'

The second rejection led to immediate action. With Mrs Witherspoon's unfriendly words ringing in his ears, the Deputy marched straight in.

BALRAJ MEETS SOME BULLIES

In less than a second all the pupils were on their feet. But it was far from clear why they had risen. Was this to escape the boredom of the lesson? Or were they playfully teasing him? Hiding giggles, the children sat down as quickly as they had risen.

The next words of the teacher left some of the pupils gasping in surprise. 'Ah, it's you, Mr Ramsbottom. I thought it was the invisible man. You're so short I couldn't see you through the window.'

Taken aback, the Deputy said nothing for several seconds. The few remaining hairs on the back of his head rose in anger, but wisely he counted to ten before replying. By the time he replied he had already stepped out of the classroom and it was impossible to tell whether he knew he had been insulted. 'Thank you for your kindness, Mrs Witherspoon. Now I know you'll be looking forward to teaching Balraj, and so I'll leave you to welcome him.'

Left suddenly on his own, Balraj found that he was grinning uncontrollably. Waiting by Mrs Witherspoon's desk, he somehow sensed her coiled anger and his legs wobbled like jelly fresh out of a mould. The teacher, for her part, seemed to have decided to ignore him completely and she carried on talking to the class as if he didn't exist.

One or two of the children began to take pleasure in Balraj's misfortune. With faces hidden behind books or buried beneath hands, pupils at the front giggled and sniggered. Someone pretended to cough and then muttered something which caused laughter. Balraj felt more embarrassed than at any time in his life and even his nervous grin disappeared as he struggled to make sure that he didn't cry.

The amusement seemed to remind Mrs Witherspoon of the new arrival. Thumping her reading book on her desk, she glowered at the class and for the first time spoke to him directly. 'You're going to have to watch it here. I don't like boys at the best of times, except for very tall ones who can carry my bags. Now stop your silly sniffling and go and find yourself somewhere to sit.'

The only empty place was in the very back corner of the cramped room and it was far from easy to reach. 6Q were working at large flat topped tables which gobbled up most of the room. Exercise books and folders were stored in multi-coloured moveable stacks which added to the general clutter. Four or five computers on trolleys took up all the remaining space.

The chair was in the most awkward place of all, on the far side of a large rectangle made by linking three tables. Seven children were already sitting around it and Balraj had to squeeze past them all.

To make matters worse, they were not in a mood to be helpful. Some were deliberately spiteful and made no effort to move their chairs to let him through. More tears came into his eyes when, choking with embarrassment, he realised that one or two were happy to see that he was upset.

The biggest problem was a boy who also looked as though he might be new. Like Balraj, he didn't have a green Hoddle Street sweatshirt. Instead, the badge on his purple sweatshirt showed that he had until recently attended Minor Vale Middle. Unfortunately, his behaviour suggested that there was no possibility of friendship.

Sensing hostility, Balraj timidly muttered 'Excuse me' as he tried to squeeze by him. This courtesy fell on unsympathetic ears for, as he made his uncertain movement, the boy stuck out his leg spitefully from underneath the table. The effect was immediate. Tumbling to one side, Balraj disturbed piles of dusty textbooks stacked on the edge of a computer trolley. Like toy soldiers hit by a marble, the books fell one by one onto the floor. Around the room children smirked and giggled and the bully muttered an insult from somewhere behind an ink covered fist.

'If you would be kind enough to stop snivelling for a moment, I'd be able to get on with my lesson,' snorted Mrs Witherspoon from the front of the room.

For the first time in his life, Balraj felt completely and utterly alone. Glancing up at the clock behind the teacher's table, he saw that it was only 11.40 a.m. At least twenty more painful minutes would have to pass before he would be saved by the bell.

Nothing in all his happy years at Sweeton Combined School had prepared Balraj for the situation he now found himself in.

BALRAJ MEETS SOME BULLIES

What do you do when a ferocious teacher decides to talk for the whole lesson?

The class seemed to know the answer. As Mrs Witherspoon read, only her own dull voice and the occasional creaking of a chair disturbed the silence. All heads faced downwards as if reading stories written in invisible ink on the smoothly polished tables.

Balraj copied the position. At least it gave him a good chance to think! He could not believe how quickly life had changed. One day he had been living happily 'up north' and the next he had been moved to the opposite end of the country to stay with his aunt and uncle. Balraj had known for weeks about his parents' long awaited visit to India. The trip, planned perfectly to occupy weeks when their own shop in Sweeton was being re-fitted, would give time to visit grandparents and sort out important family business. His big sister, Satinder, had known all along that she would be flying out and Balraj had taken it for granted that he, too, would soon be soaring through the sky.

But how wrong he had been! With SATs coming up, his parents had reluctantly decided to leave him behind and to make matters worse they had kept this secret until the very last moment. It was only during the traffic-jam-punctuated journey down the M6 that Balraj learnt he was to stay in Bridley whilst the rest of the family were overseas.

Balraj liked his aunt and uncle. But Bridley was over 250 kilometres from Sweeton and he had never stayed with them before. Uncle Sukhdeep was much older than his own dad and all but one of his aunt's and uncle's children had already left home. Big cousin Hardeep would certainly be good for the occasional game of cricket but he would be far too busy at college most of the time.

How Balraj had cried when he first learnt of the plan. When he was younger that would have done the trick. But the car hadn't stopped. Nowadays there was no changing his parents' minds when they had decided that something was for the best.

By the end of his first morning at Hoddle Street, however, he had already come to realise that Mrs Witherspoon's class would certainly not be 'for the best'.

FOUR: BALRAJ MAKES A FRIEND

It was not until several minutes after the sounding of the lunchtime bell that Mrs Witherspoon dismissed her captives. Balraj shot out of the classroom. Barely stopping to grab his coat from its resting place on a corridor peg, he followed his fast-moving classmates. Unfortunately, once outside, the pleasure of freedom soon turned to gloom. Nobody spoke to him. Unsure what to do, he stood on the edge of a crowded playground and watched as everyone else began to play. Some were playing football and patball. For others, chasing games were definitely the order of the day: Stuck in the Mud, Forty Forty, Chain Tig. How he longed to join in!

Balraj wandered over to the fence which marked the boundary between Hoddle Street Juniors and Pixy Infants. Tiny heads were poking through all the available gaps as four and five year olds chattered excitedly to big brothers and sisters. The happy scene made him feel worse, turning his thoughts to his own loneliness. Why hadn't his mum and dad taken him? It was all so unfair. Satinder was taking her GCSEs at the end of the year. But they had taken her for the first part of the trip. Why were things always so different for her?

The shrill blast of a whistle announced the arrival of a lunchtime supervisor. Dressed in a yellow overall, she shrieked, 'Time for dinner, Year 6. Line up.' Scuffing his shoes and kicking sadly at loose bits of tarmac, he joined the back of the queue.

At least the supervisor seemed nice! In her oversized jacket, she looked for all the world like an enormous lemon sherbert. And she seemed to know how to keep everyone in a good mood. Walking constantly up and down the line, and occasionally funnelling groups through the doorway into the canteen, she had a kind word for everyone. Her name, as far as Balraj could tell, was Doreen. Tossing her head back and revealing smiling brown eyes, she even told a football joke. It was one heard many times before, but somehow the way she told it made it funnier than ever. 'Why do they train astronauts at Banchester United?' she asked, with mock puzzlement. 'Because there's no atmosphere, Doreen,' chorused half the queue in reply.

Reaching the end of the line, Doreen stopped. Large brown eyes seemed suddenly serious. ' Hey ducks, you're a sad looking little bunny. New here? On your own? This sad situation ain't right. No way! Whose class are you in anyway, darling? 6Q?'

Doreen turned and singled out someone towards the front of the queue. ' Marcus, this little kid's lonely. Do something useful for once! Look after him for me, will you, Netball Post?'

'For the lady with more jokes than a box of last year's Christmas crackers, I'll do anything,' came the good humoured reply. Smiling confidently, Marcus's long legs took giant strides as he danced down the line. Grabbing Balraj by the arm, he sped back to his own position near the front of the queue.

The focus now of unexpected attention, the newcomer felt more embarrassed than ever. With all eyes upon him, he felt out of place like a sweet perched on the edge of a dentist's chair.

It was fortunate, therefore, that Marcus was so determined to cheer him up. 'Are you liking it in Witherboot's class, man?' he shouted above the noise of the queue. Still shy, Balraj found it difficult to know what to say. At last he found his tongue. 'She's not exactly a bundle of laughs,' he whispered uncertainly. The answer seemed to please Marcus who chuckled for a moment before replying. 'Yes, man, that's cool. Not exactly a bundle of laughs!' Balraj smiled in return, safe now in the knowledge that after dinner there would be at least one friendly face in the classroom.

The queue moved forward, snaking its way between two open glass doors which led into a crowded dining hall. Soon a comforting smell of chips filled the air. But just as the boys reached the doorway, the queue came to a halt. 'Out of chips again, no doubt,' murmured Marcus.

Irritated by the delay, one or two children continued to push forward and as they did so someone started to kick at the back of Balraj's legs. Turning around abruptly the little newcomer saw a purple sweatshirt and instantly knew who was trying to provoke him.

This time Balraj reacted without thinking. Ignoring the bully's greater height, he pushed him away and raised his fists. But before blows could be exchanged, Marcus stepped between them. Taking hold of the bully's sweatshirt, he pulled him sharply forwards towards his own face. In a strong voice which everyone could hear, he shouted, 'Look, Bernard, you've been with us for two weeks now. But you're picking on my little friend. How long before you learn we don't put up with this here?' Suddenly Marcus released the bully and spoke more calmly. 'Were it not for the fact that I gave up fighting years ago, I would sort you out myself. As it is, I'll keep my glasses on, save my fists the trouble, and have a word with Ramsbottom instead.'

The promise was kept. Inside the dining hall, Marcus marched straight over to the Deputy who was stacking piles of metal trays by the serving hatch. Seconds later, and looking extremely crestfallen, Bernard left the dining hall ready to wait outside the Deputy's office until there was 'time to talk things over'.

From the self service counter, Balraj chose one of his favourite meals: a double portion of chips, cheese pie, baked beans. Marcus continued to talk cheerfully, claiming that Hoddle Street was the best school in town. Conversation turned to Mrs Witherspoon. 'Not bad either, really,' claimed Marcus, somewhat recklessly. 'I reckon she's just a bit worked up because they think inspectors from ROFTOT will be here soon,' he added.

Shyly Balraj grinned, bit into a chip, and made no reply.

FIVE: BAD NEWS?

A pleasant bubble of excitement in classrooms throughout the school signalled that the school day was drawing to a close. Down in 3T, Alan watched, quietly satisfied, as trays were tidied, chairs lifted onto tables and children smiled their goodbyes. Then, pleased to see that everyone had remembered to take their coats, the Deputy hurried to the staffroom. He was keen to snatch a cup of tea. After teaching Year 3, his throat felt as dry as the Sahara Desert!

There was just enough time to ring Jed Langley whilst waiting for the kettle to boil. All afternoon, fears about what the Bridley Town Youth Team coach might say had been lurking in the back of Alan's mind. Would he have good news, as Sally seemed to think? Somehow the Deputy doubted it. He pessimistically imagined Jed's words. 'It is with much regret that Bridley Town have reluctantly decided against using Hoddle Street Juniors on the day of the grand opening of our new all-seater stadium.'

Alan picked up the 'phone nervously. For two minutes the steaming kettle received no attention. Keen to make sure that he had got the message accurately, Alan jotted down some notes: Bridley Town's new stadium, a Year 6 match, opponents Anniversary Lane Primary, boys and girls in both teams.

Seconds later the Deputy hurried from the staffroom carrying a mug of piping hot tea. Glancing at his watch rather anxiously now, he recognised that he was a little late for Ms Granger's meeting.

No Monday at Hoddle Street could ever be complete without a gathering of the senior management team. And there was no doubt at all that Alan really did need to hurry. Ms Granger liked meetings but hated lateness. Each week she waited, carefully noting when her colleagues arrived. Robin Johnstone, the gloomy Head of Upper School, was always first; Mrs Hussain, the bubbly Head of Lower School, would appear a second or two later. And last of all would be Alan, muttering incomprehensible apologies and armed with a gigantic mug of tea.

In recent times, management meetings had been held over in Ms Granger's new Administration Block, a smart office complex which was some distance from the main school building. This was a big change from the time of 'Blaster' Bullcock. In her day, the office had looked out onto the large playground used by all but the smallest children. At playtime 'Blaster' had watched constantly, convincing generations of pupils that her small green eyes possessed strange telescopic powers. For years, the slightest hint of a playground quarrel had resulted in a deadly blast of her ship's foghorn voice through her ever open window.

Older children still looked back with fond memories to the days of the 'Blaster'. The corridor outside her room had always been so full of life, a place filled with happy chatter and the smell of antiseptic. Her office had constantly welcomed a stream of visitors: little people from Year 3 proudly clutching papier mâché dinosaurs; and older Year 6 pupils with complex mathematical investigations tucked neatly underneath their arm.

Children were rarely allowed to visit Ms Granger's new office complex. Completed ahead of schedule during the summer holidays, it had been in full use ever since the start of term. But, like a General disclosing an important military secret, the new Headteacher had recently announced that the new Administration Block would be officially opened by the Mayor of Bridley on the second Friday in November. Somewhat mysteriously, she had then surprised everyone by suggesting that the opening ceremony would involve at least 100 flags as well as all 600 children in the school.

Teachers wondered whether the position of the office complex told them anything about Ms Granger. Separated from the main building by both a lawn and a pathway, the Administration Block was a remarkably long way from all the classrooms. Mrs Hussain silently asked herself whether the Headteacher had a mystery illness which made her allergic to children, whilst Robin Johnstone thought that, in the manner of a First World War General, the new Head planned to lead from the rear. But it was Leroy Jones, specialist science teacher and classroom wit, who was perhaps closest to the mark. He had nicknamed the building 'Mission Control' in recognition of Ms Granger's ability to run the school well from a remote distance.

Outside Mission Control was a large notice. It read 'WELCOME! Ring once for the secretary. Ring twice for Ms Granger.' To save Sally an unnecessary journey, Alan pressed the secret combination which opened the door automatically.

Rubber plants seemed to cover every available surface in the short corridor between the General Office and Ms Granger's room. Like an explorer heading bravely into a rainforest, Alan successfully negotiated his way between the plants and entered the room. 'Sorry I'm late. I've been gasping for a cuppa all afternoon. But when I nipped to the staffroom I found that some idiot had turned the kettle off.'

' I turned it off,' replied Ms Granger, rather crossly. ' I can't be doing with all this time wasting. How can improvement targets be reached with such a casual attitude?'

The meeting settled down. Always first to arrive and always first asleep, Robin Johnstone, had, as usual, claimed the most comfortable chair. The only time he moves quickly is when he rushes to get here first, thought Alan. However, with the combination of the heavy scent of flowering plants and the warmth of the room, the Deputy, too, found that it was far from easy to pay attention. Through an open window, the faint sound of the cleaners chattering cheerfully over in the main building ebbed and flowed like an ever more distant tide as Ms Granger moved through each agenda item.

After several minutes teetering on the edge of blissful sleep, Alan suddenly became far more alert. Ms Granger had uttered the magic word 'football'. What had she said? Unfortunately, the Headteacher was holding a broken coffee mug and so Alan knew at once that her words would not be words of pleasure.

'You no doubt all know by now that I hate football,' said Ms Granger. 'I'm sure all of you agree that it's because there's far too much sport on television that boys don't do enough reading. And footballs, as Miss Cooper discovered to her cost, cause accidents. Today, therefore, I've had to make some important decisions. For the moment football training for the school team can continue. However, I've spoken to the Upper School and I have banned football in the playground.'

Ms Granger paused for a moment, allowing time for her words to sink in. Then, turning theatrically to her desk, she picked up a series of notices. 'Alan, you are to put these up around school before you go home tonight.'

NO FOOTBALLS IN SCHOOL
NO BALL GAMES IN THIS PLAYGROUND
TALK NOT PLAY IS THE 'GOOD SCHOOL' WAY

The Deputy's mouth opened like a toad gulping air. But, recognising that Ms Granger had made up her mind, he said nothing.

Almost at once the magic word *football* turned his thoughts in a far happier direction by reminding him of his conversation with Jed Langley. Their conversation had brought remarkable news: Bridley Town F.C. were now definitely going to use Hoddle Street's Year 6 side on the day of the grand opening of their new all-seater stadium. Brilliant!

Yet even such happy thoughts as these soon plunged to earth when Ms Granger dropped her next bombshell. Her words at first seemed designed to tease. 'Now I've got what I'm sure you will all agree is some wonderful news and so you all must listen carefully.' She hesitated before continuing.

Alan recognised it was time to wake up Robin Johnstone, who slept on with the peaceful smile of a pensioner dreaming of deck chairs and ice cream. Anxious to alert his friend, Alan silently kicked the back of the easy chair until Robin gathered in his legs like a spider fearing an attack and listened.

'The news is, as I was saying, very good indeed,' continued Ms Granger. 'This afternoon I received a call from ROFTOT, the Regional Office for Training of Teachers.'

'Regional Office for Telling off Teachers,' muttered Robin gloomily.

Turning a deaf ear, Ms Granger continued. 'I'm delighted to say that I've been able to bring the inspection forward. As you know, I'm an inspector myself and I'm really looking forward to hearing what our visitors will discover when they arrive here straight after half term.' Bombshell dropped, the young Headteacher stood up and declared the meeting closed.

SIX: NOT FAIR!

The main school building was already empty by the time Alan Ramsbottom returned to his office to collect his bags and car keys. Only the irregular metallic coughs from somewhere deep within the central heating system disturbed the silence. The Deputy glanced out at the darkening sky, shivered, and closed a small window.

It was a pity that Doris the cleaner had already gone. He always enjoyed their conversations and more than anyone else at Hoddle Street she could bring a smile to his face.

There were many signs that Doris had recently been in the room. The dull green carpet had that freshly hoovered look which reminded him of a cricket pitch ready for the first ball in a Test match. The sharp smell of lemon-scented polish still filled the air. Loose papers scattered on his desk were now piled in his in-tray.

Doris had left a message:

Sorry I missed you today, Mr Ramsbottom. I found lots of little notes on your desk when I came in. I've put them in your bag. I think some boys were looking for you at the end of the day.

The Deputy put on his anorak, insulated his cold, bald head in his warm flat cap and hurried to his car. His route home took him along the narrow, winding streets in the middle of Bridley and then on towards the outskirts of town.

As so often, his mind went over the events of the day. What a mess he'd made of taking that new boy to Mrs Witherspoon's class. But what good news from Jed Langley. Imagine! Hoddle Street Juniors to play in a match at Bridley Town! Then his thoughts turned to the day's big news. ROFTOT inspectors in school in two weeks' time. He did a quick mental calculation … Yes, that really did mean just four school days and the half term holiday to get ready.

When he reached the outskirts of town, he turned out onto the main road which headed off in the direction of Woodgrave, the village in which the Ramsbottoms had now lived for so many years. As usual, he looked over to the right. Work on Bridley Town's new stadium was now almost finished. A lifelong supporter, he could even remember the glory days when Bridley had been in the top division.

The traffic lights outside the ground turned to red and for a few precious moments he was able to look at the work more closely. Even from outside, the new stadium was most impressive.

Someone was testing the floodlights. At the club's old ground the light shone down from four mighty pylons. But now things had changed. The new floodlights were far smaller and had been set at regular intervals along the roof of the main stand. They were working well. A great crest of light arched upwards, transforming the late afternoon darkness. With so much work now finished, the ground really would be ready in time for the opening friendly against Banchester United.

The traffic lights turned to green and Alan picked up speed. Thinking of football again! He laughed silently, imagining what Mavis, his wife, would say. 'Is sport the only thing you think about?' she often asked.

What, he wondered, would she say if she knew that he secretly wished that he had played far more football when he was young and fit? An apprentice player with Bridley Town for a short time as a teenager, Alan had actually played very little football during those key years when his own children were growing up. Now in his early fifties, he would still wait near his phone each Friday evening just in case one of the many teams he had played for over the years suddenly found themselves short of a player.

Mavis thought he was eccentric. But, in fairness, this was because she had never been able to get over the present he had made for Gary, their youngest child and only son, on his third birthday. The problem had, perhaps, not been the gift itself – goalposts. But what about the size? Two full sized goalposts for a three year old to use in the back garden of a small semi had always seemed slightly over the top.

Mavis remembered it all so well. In a sudden burst of energy, linked to the start of Hoddle Street Juniors' summer holidays, Alan had visited a local DIY store. His purchases included four large fencing posts to use as uprights and two 8 metre lengths of hardwood for crossbars. This was not a good idea. Even with seats adjusted and all windows open, the crossbars were far too long to move in their mini! Result? With crossbars precariously balanced on top of a borrowed wheelbarrow, Mavis spent a long, hot and embarrassing afternoon helping her husband get all his wood home.

For one long and memorable week the goalposts attracted constant attention. First thing Monday morning a photographer from the Bridley Evening News turned up and took a picture of Alan and the tiny Gary. Both were smartly turned out in new football kits generously donated by Bridley Town in a clever publicity stunt. But it was all so embarrassing for Mavis; and the photograph of Alan's knobbly and wobbly knees had even attracted two letters of complaint.

The main problem, however, was that everybody wanted to use the goalposts. For a week a constant stream of children knocked on their door demanding the right to play whilst somehow conveniently forgetting that they were talking about posts *in Mavis's back garden* and not in the public park.

The final straw came during the hot and dusty Friday afternoon. Returning from her part time job down at the Post Office, Mavis found Alan and most of the local church team in the middle of a match!

She judged her moment well. That evening, when Alan had gone out jogging, she took a spade from the garden shed and dug up the posts, attracting a sympathetic round of applause from neighbours watering plants in nearby gardens.

Yes, Mavis does think I'm eccentric, thought Alan, as he parked his car in the driveway of their country cottage. But when we sit down later on she'll still be anxious to hear how Gary has got on in tonight's Banchester United match.

Without further thought, he settled into the end of day routine which had become so familiar since their children had finally left home. First of all, he popped outside to feed the rabbit. Upon seeing his fresh bowl of grain, old Bob took advantage and nipped out of the hutch into his run. Like a youngster still eager to escape, he playfully burrowed in the corner. For a while Alan stroked him until, quietly satisfied, Bob turned and hopped back into his hutch.

With the rabbit fed and watered, Alan started to cater for adult needs. He turned on the radio and caught the last few minutes of the 6 o'clock news as he prepared the evening meal. Aware nowadays of the need to try to eat healthily, he prepared a simple meal: baked potato, tuna fish and broccoli. As usual on week days, he ate alone. Since becoming a successful barrister Mavis had hardly ever returned home before 8pm.

Alan washed his meal down with a glass of lime juice and went into his study. Never the most enthusiastic marker of exercise books, he was always keen to get this job out of the way. For an hour or so he sat at his desk as his red pen worked its way from page to page. At last he was able to turn off his desk lamp with an air of quiet satisfaction. He wandered into the lounge carrying the loose bundle of notes which Doris had put into his bag.

The radio was tuned into 'Sport on 9'. Sitting back comfortably in the ample cushions of his favourite armchair, he listened as scores and progress reports came in from grounds around the country. Bridley Town had no match and so Alan most wanted to hear the score from the game between Lobon City and Banchester United.

He smiled happily when he heard the good news he had longed to hear ever since the start of the season way back in August. Not only was there to be full second half coverage of the Banchester match, but Reg Francis announced that Gary Ramsbottom would play the full second half. The Deputy's 20 year old son had finally succeeded in getting into the Banchester first team!

Reg Francis's high pitched voice continued: 'Gary Ramsbottom, recently signed from second division Bridley Town, is not the most skilful of players but you can't fault him for commitment. I'm sure he'll add a new dimension to the Banchester attack after such a dull first half performance.'

With one ear now firmly on the radio, Alan tried to settle back to his remaining jobs. He started to read through the notes Doris had put in his bag but had to stop for a moment when Mavis popped her head round the door to say that she was back from work. How many times had he heard the words which came next? 'Just need to go into my study for a while, dear. I'll catch your news later when we have our drinking chocolate.'

Reg Francis' voice went ever higher like a choirboy singing descant. Reaching fever pitch, he emphasised that Banchester looked like scoring because Gary Ramsbottom had given their attack 'an extra bit of bite'.

Yet, much to his surprise, Alan found that the notes Doris had placed so carefully inside his bag were beginning to take his attention away from the football. He flicked through the pile once again. There were, he reckoned, 47 notes in total and all but two were from children worried that footballs would soon be banned in the playground.

Mandeep 5R
What will we do? Stand in the playground for an hour?
Jack and Tommy 5Z
We want to improve our reading. But that will be very hard if we can't play football.
Leroy 6X
It's very boring when there are no ball games
Michael 6Q
Your own son signed for Banchester United. I bet you let him play football when he was young, sir.
Ruth and Michelle 6W
We think it will be very sexist if Ms Granger bans footballs. Just because she doesn't like football she wants to stop kids playing games they like.
All the children in 5W
Please can you help us, sir? We know you like football, sir. And we used to watch your son when he played for Bridley Town.

PS We hope Gary will be in Banchester's first team soon. We are looking forward to watching him on 'Match of the Day'!

Alan wondered what he should do. The letters struck a raw nerve because he always liked to see plenty of games in the playground. And what would all the children think when they found out that Ms Granger had decided to ban *all* balls, and not just footballs, from the playground? But he also knew that Ms Granger had a point. Two or three children as well as Miss Cooper had been upset by accidents in the playgrounds in recent weeks. There were times when he was glad he had never been a Headteacher.

Alan reached the end of the pile. Somehow the last note looked different and he hesitated for a moment before picking it up. It was clearly nothing to do with football. Instead, it was a rough copy of a letter to some parents.

Dear Dad and Mum,

I've had a bad day. My teacher is horrible and I think she is a bit of a bully. There is also a nasty boy called Bernard in my class. A nice boy called Marcus is my friend. The Deputy Headteacher is a bit old and dozy but might be okay. He lost me and the music teacher made me carry everything.

I'm missing you. When will you be back?

Balraj

SEVEN: ARE WE READY?

'We've really got to get cracking,' said Leroy Jones, looking at the staffroom notice board. 'There's no doubt we've got to get cracking straight away.' As he repeated his words other teachers arrived, eager to check on the rumour that had circulated so quickly. He looked at the board again and read out Ms Granger's notice.

We welcome the ROFTOT Inspection team to school immediately after half term. Make sure your rooms are ready!

Frantic activity followed. In classrooms all around the school children got stuck into a hundred and one important tasks: sharpening pencils, tidying work trays and sorting out Book Corners. Old jam jars and paint brushes hidden away since the days when classes had Art every week were washed and cleaned.

Tom, the schoolkeeper, also caught the mood of excitement. Stocky and slow of foot he always worked at his own pace. But suddenly he found more energy. Dressed in smart overalls, and with a pencil carefully balanced between the top of his ear and his mop of silvery grey hair, he set about a thousand and one unfinished tasks. Broken chairs were fixed, missing batteries placed in clocks and wooden floors polished until they shone like coins leaving the Royal Mint. Indeed, as early as Tuesday afternoon, he was polishing the main corridor with so much enthusiasm that some children started to expect a royal visitor.

Ms Granger worked with great authority. Dressed in a new grey suit, and somehow maintaining her balance on the highest of heels, she moved from room to room making notes on her clipboard. One minute she would turn up in a Year Five classroom keen to borrow teams of helpers, the next she would be down in the canteen explaining the special dietary requirements of the inspection team.

Each day Ms Granger left a stream of thoughtful messages on Alan's desk. But on Wednesday afternoon he found a note which took him completely by surprise.

Alan – Kindly make sure that you are in school by 6 am tomorrow. You will not be disappointed.

First thing Thursday morning, Alan left home early, as instructed. Before even turning into the car park, he could see that Ms Granger was already waiting by the school gate. Parked nearby was a large pick-up truck. Two workmen, both of whom looked as if they had recently been extremely busy, were leaning against its side.

The Deputy looked around for further signs of activity. A large hole had been dug outside the offices. More mysteriously, the rectangle of grass which separated the school hall and car park was now peppered by a series of much smaller holes.

Ms Granger was excited. 'Delighted to see you, Alan,' she said in an uncharacteristically bright and breezy manner. She clapped her hands and turned her attention to the workmen, 'Okay lads, over to you.' At this command the workmen sauntered to the back of the pick-up and gently lowered a long flagpole into the hole outside the Administration Block. Task completed, the workmen whistled and shouted, 'Right, Freda'. With that, the peace of the early morning was shattered by a shrill warning bleep as the cement mixer reversed into the school grounds.

Soon the driver had skilfully backed up to the hole. She popped her head out of the driver's cab, carefully checked her position and then slowly released a stream of cement mix. Within no time the hole was full. With a cheery wave she left the school grounds, her work mates following seconds later in the pick-up truck.

'I know you'll like this,' said Ms Granger as the vehicles left. 'I've decided that we should always have a flag on display outside my office. When I've got more money I'll buy flags for other countries. I'm sure ROFTOT will like it.'

During Thursday morning the wave of excitement now sweeping the school grew far more intense. Suddenly anxious to ensure that all display work was absolutely up to date, some teachers started to replace the beautiful wall displays which had been prepared so carefully just before the start of term. Soon waste paper was everywhere and a call had to go out for extra bin bags.

It was at this stage, with all practice SATs out of the way, that Year 6 really got involved. The sniff of a chance to get out of lessons led to many 'helpful' suggestions. Never short of a good idea, Marcus was one of the first off the mark, sprinting down to see Alan Ramsbottom with an interesting suggestion. The spare classroom behind the canteen hadn't been used for five years or more but needed tidying. Marcus offered to do it. The Deputy was very puzzled by his chosen helpers – Bernard Finlay and Balraj Singh seemed an odd combination. Even so, he gladly accepted the boys' offer to do some 'spring cleaning'.

The Lewis twins were next to see the Deputy. Again, he was delighted when they volunteered to move the bin bags in each classroom. Freckled, ginger-haired and totally reliable, the girls could be trusted to do any job well.

Unfortunately, in this life things do not always go as planned. Soon the girls found that their job was far harder and heavier than expected and so, like the good science pupils they were, they started to think of ways to save energy.

It was hardly surprising, since she was older by two minutes, that it was Philippa who came up with the plan of action. But it was most unfortunate that they failed to get permission from Felicity Brown, the school's part time gardener. Busily at work gathering autumn leaves she naturally missed her wheelbarrow almost immediately. If only they had taken the trouble to ask, the girls would have learnt that the wheelbarrow was unsuitable for their task. With its flat, wobbly and rather lop-sided front wheel the barrow seemed to have a mind of its own. Going from room to room, the girls soon discovered that it was as hard to steer as a single-minded supermarket trolley.

What a pity that nobody was following the girls! From behind, the muddy trail snaking its way from room to room was easy to see. Someone might even have spotted the other problem – the insect problem – which made matters so much worse. For the wheelbarrow had been full of leaf mould in the recent past. And suddenly, cruelly cut off from their cosy habitat, an almost liquid stream of centipedes, millipedes, earwigs and woodlice was slipping and slithering along the beautifully polished corridors as the insects set off to find new homes.

It was fully 4 p.m. before Alan discovered that all was not well. Called to the medical room, he learnt first of Ms Granger's unfortunate accident. With clipboard in one hand and stopwatch in the other, she had been happily timing support assistants taking down wall displays when misfortune arrived. In their haste to complete their job before the end of day, and pushing the wheelbarrow at a speed worthy of a grand prix race track, the Lewis twins had turned a corner at great speed and bumped into Ms Granger.

Worse followed. Whilst Ms Granger's ankle was being bandaged, Alan tried to offer words of comfort. But the peace of the school building shattered like a milk bottle hitting concrete the second Tom returned to see the cleaners. Fully awake after a well deserved afternoon nap over in his schoolkeeper's flat, he was utterly perplexed. What had happened? Had the school been invaded by an army of snails? Why were woodlice on the loose? Why, above all, were his beautifully polished corridors coated in mud?

It was hard to tell who was the more annoyed. Tom did not calm down at all until two of the cleaners arrived with mops and bucket. Ms Granger also failed to see the funny side of things, although she calmed down a great deal as soon as her ankle was fully bandaged.

It was fortunate that Sally was her usual tower of strength. Without even waiting to be asked, she made three cups of coffee as soon as she had completed her first aid. Then, with no grumbling at all, even though she was already late, she waved cheerily as she guided her wheelchair through the swing doors and set off home.

At precisely this moment Alan remembered his interesting news – the good news which would help to keep Ms Granger's mind off her injury. As soon as they had drunk their coffee, Alan marched out of the office with the enthusiasm of a new army recruit, inviting Tom and Ms Granger to follow.

Once back in the main building, the Deputy sped through the hall and hurried through the dining area before eventually stopping in the spare classroom behind the kitchens. The room was empty apart from three old wooden desks arranged in a neat row in front of an even older blackboard. It was dusty and Alan coughed asthmatically as soon as he tried to speak.

'Just come and see what's in here,' he wheezed. 'Three boys from 6Q cleaned this out this afternoon and they made an exciting discovery.'

'Don't be daft, lad. They've found nowt new,' murmured Tom playfully. But before he could continue, the Deputy interrupted. 'No, don't spoil it for Ms Granger, come over and have a look for yourself.' Then, without even allowing time for Ms Granger to limp across the room, he reached up and took the board off the wall.

The Headteacher stared in amazement for it was clear that the board covered a large hole in the wall. She started to hobble forward keen to take a much closer look, but as she did so Tom interrupted, words spilling out ten to the dozen.

'The lad's losing 'is memory! He's only 'found' the old P.E. Cupboard. And it's not really been lost. Door's round t'other side. Mind you t'as bin hid by wallpaper from when Bridley Council painted school. Reckon that were abaht ten years ago. T'is funny nobody's bothered till now. Reckon there must be good gear in there left from when this were a middle school. Take you in tomorrow when it's light.'

Back in his office, Alan collected his coat and got ready for home. Just before he left, Doris popped her head round his door.
'Where have you been hiding away, Alan? Marcus and those new boys what have been sorting out were looking for you after school. They grunted something about finding a box but in the end they went home. I've put it under your desk. Might be full of gold! See you tomorrow.'

EIGHT: MAVIS AND THE BOX

The mouldy cardboard box on the back seat made Alan regret that curiosity had got the better of him. Long before reaching home, his car smelt like a blocked drain on a hot summer's day. When at last he turned into the driveway of Primrose Cottage, he felt as relieved as the manager of a football team escaping relegation on the last day of the season. He hopped out of the car and hurried inside, delighted to leave the box behind.

It took no time at all to get tea ready. As usual, he ate alone once he had checked that old Bob was okay. What, he wondered, would Mavis make of tonight's meal? His own stomach felt most uneasy. Rice, radish and tinned sardines took very little effort, but it would be the first meal crossed off his list when the long awaited retirement day eventually arrived.

His thoughts returned to the cupboard. From his own quick inspection it was clear that it contained some wonderful surprises. Unless his own eyes were starting to deceive him, he had seen some great tennis rackets. Old and wooden they certainly were, but even so they were far superior to the cheap plastic rackets now used at the school's tennis club. If time allowed tomorrow, he would certainly take a closer look.

But what of the box? Clearly it must contain something very special indeed, for otherwise the boys would not have wanted to show it him.

With such thoughts in mind, Alan could curb his curiosity no longer. Without putting on his anorak, even though it was raining quite heavily, he hurried out to the car. Coughing repeatedly, he carried the box into the cottage. Then, anxious not to spread the smell, he put it down in the hallway.

He took a closer look. Noticing that there appeared to be some faint writing on its sides, he used the sleeve of his jumper to wipe off some of the mould until the words could be read more easily. They took him by surprise and carried him back to his own childhood:

Ramsbottom tomato soup
Soup for the top group
Eat with white bread
And your face will turn red.

He smiled. In his own childhood he had often had a nice slice of white bread and a bowl of Ramsbottom for tea. His mother had joked that the family owned a soup factory, but of course that hadn't been true. The box had to be very old indeed. As far as he could remember, Ramsbottom Liquid Soup Enterprises had been bought out by a larger company when he was still a boy.

Alan was keen to investigate further. With all the care of a surgeon performing a delicate operation, he lifted the fragile lid in anticipation. But then came a wave of disappointment – the box was full of old netball bibs!

For a moment he wondered why the boys had bothered to put it in his office. Probably, he reflected, it had been the first place they had reached. At least they had solved a long lasting mystery. The school had often seemed short of games equipment in recent years. No wonder, with so many things hidden away.

The bibs were in house colours – blue, green, red and yellow – and were covered with layers of dust and fluff. Though old, they would still come in very handy. How many times had he heard Robin Johnstone grumbling in the staffroom about the shortage of blue bibs? And somehow there never were enough bibs for games lesson on Wednesday afternoons when Year 6 went outside.

Of course, the bibs would need washing and so he had to hurry. Mavis had always been a stickler about washing. 'Don't just drop it there. Soak it in the bath first,' she had been telling him for years. Pleased to have remembered her advice *before* she arrived home, he filled the bath with piping hot soapy water and dropped the bibs in.

When Mavis returned from work an hour or so later, Alan was sitting in his armchair listening to a football match on the radio. She popped her head round the door and handed him an envelope she had picked up in the hallway.

'Thanks, I was wondering where that was,' said Alan. 'Your dinner's on the table,' he added with ears glued to the radio.

'I'm off for a bath first,' responded Mavis. 'It's been a hard day.'

Listening closely to the latest goal mouth action, Alan waved vaguely in his wife's direction as she headed upstairs.

The whistle blew for half time and as Sid Butler gave the latest scores from the evening's main matches Alan turned his attention to the letter. Much to his surprise, he found that it was from Mrs Witherspoon. Its tone was less surprising. She seemed, as usual, to be annoyed.

Alan, I am not happy. Ms Granger has put TWO extra boys in my class at a very bad time in the year. Will you move them out straight away please? Give me some extra girls instead.

I can tell just by looking at them that they can't be trusted. At the end of lunch break I found them both standing in my classroom with a dirty cardboard box. Can you imagine!

The little cheeky one who spends all his time grinning claimed they were 'putting it in a safe place'. A likely story! I know they just wanted to tip the contents in my cupboard and run out to play.

Tall boys are usually a lot brighter. But I'm not happy about Bernard. He's a real pest and I insist that you put him in another class.

P.S. As you know, I don't think ALL boys are bad. Marcus is tall and nearly as bright as his sister Marlene was. He wants us to have a class discussion in circle time.

It will be about whether Year 6 should be allowed to play football at playtime. You may know that I think the ban on ball games is sensible. However, I have promised that you will come along to listen.

Regards,
Maureen

Alan found the letter puzzling and read it carefully for a second time. Even then, he was not sure what to make of it. How typical that Maureen Witherspoon was complaining about extra boys! On the other hand, the debate was a good idea. Perhaps 6Q might even have some useful suggestions.

The combination of a tummy full of salty sardines and Mrs Witherspoon's letter had made him feel rather thirsty. He took off his reading glasses and, hurrying into the kitchen, drank water from a pint-sized glass before turning on the kettle. As he waited for it to boil, he put on the rubber kitchen gloves Mavis had bought him for Christmas and started to do the dishes.

Within seconds his labours were disturbed by a sudden piercing shriek from the bathroom. Two steps at a time, he darted upstairs only to skid across a pile of dripping bibs on the wet tiles.

Mavis, standing in her fluffy pink dressing gown, spoke like a church mouse when eventually he came to a halt. 'What is that?' she asked, pointing into the murky bathwater.

Carefully side-stepping pools of water on the bathroom floor, Alan stepped forward to take a closer look. Unfortunately, the smell was sufficient to confirm that the bibs must have contained something very unpleasant indeed.

'It's a dead rat,' whispered Mavis.

White as an Alaskan Christmas, but still the brave gentleman, even when wearing his rubber kitchen gloves, the Deputy took a further step forward.

With eyes shut tight, he plunged his hand into the murky water and grabbed what appeared to be a tail.

'Only an old brush head, dear,' he said, as he regained his nerve.

NINE: A COLD, DAMP FRIDAY

The Deputy was feeling far from well. Drops of perspiration were forming on his forehead and his vest was sticking to his damp skin. He felt cold even though he had been sweating all day; every bone in his body was aching and he was beginning to wonder whether he was starting with the 'flu. Tired and slightly feverish, he would really have to struggle to get through to the end of the afternoon.

The day had been difficult. Dull, windy autumnal Fridays are never easy at the best of times and this had been one of the worst in memory. It was the kind of day when nobody wanted to step out of doors. On the playground the raw easterly wind had gone through coats more quickly than a pickpocket at the races.

Everyone was feeling miserable. For once the chasing games which had become particularly popular since footballs had been banned held little attraction. Instead, most children simply huddled together in tightly packed circles like half frozen penguins on the edge of a polar ice cap.

Feeling bored and a little cantankerous, some of the older boys turned their attention to 'play fighting'. This had never been allowed in school for a reason which was soon seen all too clearly. Within minutes a steady stream of irritable boys from Year 6 was visiting the medical room with minor cuts and bruises. Under the circumstances, it was fortunate that Mrs Maudsley, the school's part time nurse, was around, armed with cotton wool and sticking plaster.

Somewhat reluctantly, Alan went outside. He sheltered his pink ears underneath the collar of the long grey overcoat which was usually never worn before the first day in December. His presence seemed to have a settling effect. Frozen penguins started to play Stuck in the Mud and play fighting ceased as older boys started to play football with an imaginary ball.

And, as usual when out on the playground, the Deputy soon found that he was having lots of interesting conversations. First of all, children from Year 3 trotted over in twos and threes. It was amazing that so many believed that someone from the Royal Family would be visiting Hoddle Street after half term. Ms Granger really would have to put a stop to this rumour in the assembly at the end of the day.

The Lewis twins had been most sheepish. He had not quite been able to believe what they told him about the wheelbarrow fiasco. On the one hand they claimed that they hadn't noticed any mud in the corridors. On the other they said that they had noticed that the corridors were 'a bit dirty' but had been too scared to put the wheelbarrow back in the garden. Which version, he wondered, was true?

To his surprise, the chat he had most enjoyed was with Balraj and Bernard. 'Okay, sir, nice to see you, sir. This is a cool school, sir,' called out Bernard, scurrying across the playground on his drainpipe legs. Within seconds, Balraj had joined them grinning from ear to ear and keen to find out about the Year 6 Football Club. Thanks in no small measure to Marcus (and also, perhaps, to Mrs Witherspoon's aggression?) the boys now seemed to be firm friends. What a pleasant transformation from earlier in the week when Bernard's words had been so upsetting!

The whistle sounded and the Deputy watched as lines of children snaked their way back into school. At least everybody was a lot calmer now! The same could not, however, be said for Mrs Green, the music teacher. When Alan returned to his office, he found her standing outside looking as desperate as a spectator who had lost a ticket to the World Cup Final. She had, apparently, had a very difficult lunch break. Keen to find something to do, and anxious to get in out of the cold, over 200 children had turned up for recorder group. Under the circumstances, it was far from surprising that she was demanding to know when Ms Granger would begin to allow footballs in the playground again.

Alan took off his overcoat. Mrs Green's complaint had reminded him that he must hurry down to 6Q. Still shivering, the last thing he wanted to do was watch a lesson but Mrs Witherspoon was expecting him for her class debate.

He felt in his pocket, took out his handkerchief, and wiped cold sweat from his forehead. At the same time he found a crumpled note which someone from Year 3 had given him in the corridor.

Dear Mr Ramsbottom,
Kindly let me know which day the Queen will be visiting school. I want Tracey to wear her best dress.
Thanks
Joan Wright

Without further delay, Alan hurried down to 6Q's classroom. Not expecting to see any changes here, he soon had one or two surprises. The notice on the door, or rather, the NEW notice on the door, was surrounded by lots of stick-on smiley faces.

6Q IS WORKING VERY HARD TO GET HIGH SATS SCORES BUT WE ARE ALWAYS DELIGHTED WHEN VISITORS CALL!
PLEASE DON'T KNOCK - JUST WALK STRAIGHT IN AND JOIN US!

The class were already sitting in their circle and so Alan flopped down into the nearest empty chair to the door. Rather grudgingly, he had to admit to himself that, when she wanted, Mrs Witherspoon knew how to get her class talking.

6Q had borrowed a large drumstick from the Music Hut and each time someone spoke they used it as a 'microphone'. The Deputy listened, fascinated to hear their views and keen to see whether Mrs Witherspoon would listen to everybody.

Marcus was on his feet. With drumstick in hand, he was enjoying his chance to have his say. It was hard to tell whether he was trying to 'wind up' some of the girls or whether he meant his words.

'Banning footballs is very sexist and very unfair on boys, Miss,' announced Marcus boldly. 'Scientists can show that boys love anything to do with space and shape. And anyway, Miss, do you remember that picture in the book when we did about the Aztecs? Their young men used to play a game a bit like squash or tennis. At the moment we can't even play patball. This is okay for girls but it's *very unfair on boys,* Miss.'

All the class laughed and watched in eager anticipation as the drumstick was handed to Charmaine Bradley, the centre forward from Hoddle Street's mixed U.11 football team. She winked at Marcus before speaking.

'It's not exactly sexist, Miss, like, because nobody can play, like, and loads of girls like football nowadays, Miss. It's not sexist, but it is *unfair*. Like, it's just boring and cold outside now, Miss.'

The classroom door was slightly open, allowing a wintry draught to enter. Even so, the discussion held everybody's full attention. Everyone had a great deal to say as the drumstick passed around the full circle and finally reached Bernard and Balraj. Bernard took hold of the drumstick. Rocking back uncertainly on his chair, he struggled as if trying to work out what to say. Then, apparently still unsure, he simply twiddled the drumstick between long matchstick fingers before muttering 'pass' and handing it on to Balraj.

At once everybody could see that Balraj disliked speaking in front of a large group. The nervous grin which irritated Mrs Witherspoon so much returned the second he grasped the drumstick. 'For goodness sake, say something or give it back to me,' sighed Mrs Witherspoon.

Yet Balraj was determined to have his say. For an uncomfortable moment he clasped the drumstick to his pigeon chest and organised his thoughts.

'Come on and speak up,' warned Mrs Witherspoon sternly, half a second before Balraj at last found his tongue.

'It's not fair on kids who are good players, Miss,' said Balraj slowly. 'They need to practise every day, Miss. And anyway, Miss, I'm a good player, Miss, but I've hardly played at all here. The only football here now is the training for the school team. And even that's only twice a week!'

Glancing up somewhat shyly, Balraj noticed that Mrs Witherspoon was frowning and hurried to his main point. 'There's a dead simple answer, Miss. My last school bought some of those soft footballs like great big marshmallows. When you use them on a crowded playground nobody gets hurt. This school should buy some.'

'You'd talk a lot more sense if you got rid of that silly grin,' grunted Mrs Witherspoon suddenly, reaching over to take hold of the drumstick and draw Circle Time to a close.

Alan Ramsbottom avoided her eye and slipped quietly out of the room to go to assembly.

All the long side windows in the school hall were already hidden beneath a thick coating of condensation by the time classes gathered for the special assembly to mark the beginning of the half term break. Arriving with her Year 3 class, Mrs Hussain took one look at the gloom outside before closing the curtains. At the front of the hall Mrs Green played the piano as Alan directed 6Q, the last class to arrive, to its position.

When everyone had settled, Ms Granger limped to the stage clutching a large piece of card in one hand and a walking stick in the other. Her navy blue jacket and matching skirt were, as usual, immaculate. However, something was very different: for the first time since arriving at Hoddle Street she was not wearing her high heels. With one foot gently cushioned inside a pink slipper, the Headteacher managed to keep her dignity despite her difficult situation.

Leaning heavily on her walking stick, Ms Granger began to speak. Her injury had clearly not affected her voice. With the crisp, confident voice of a youthful news presenter on a minor TV channel, she explained that some 'special guests' would be in school after half term. The guests would want to hear children reading and might even watch a few lessons. Every day they would eat their dinner in the canteen and one or two would go into the playground at playtime.

Slowly and very carefully Ms Granger explained that, even though the corridors had been cleaned, the rumour that a member of the Royal Family was soon to visit Hoddle Street was wrong.

Ms Granger then lowered her voice till it was hardly above a whisper. Everyone, she insisted, must carry on exactly as normal. ('Except Mrs Witherspoon?' muttered Bernard to Balraj.)

Ms Granger paused and allowed all this important information to sink in. Next she called for her two helpers to hold up her card. From somewhere behind the piano out stepped the Lewis twins who were apparently still in the Headteacher's 'good books' in spite of the wheelbarrow fiasco. Looking as solemn as magistrates, they held the card aloft.

The Headteacher raised her walking stick and pointed at the words on the card. ' Remember,' she said, 'there will be four important 'B's when ROFTOT are here.

Be friendly
Be confident
Be helpful
Be on your best behaviour

Again, the Headteacher paused, allowing time for all this information to sink in. So that she could be absolutely sure that everyone fully understood, she asked if there were any questions.

Her eyes settled on a boy from Year 3 who had raised his arm and called out 'Miss, Miss, Miss, me, Miss.'

'Please, Miss, what time will the Queen arrive?'

For a moment Ms Granger fixed him with a glassy stare, until her eyes moved on to Belinda Pollard who also seemed to want to ask something.

'Belinda, I'm sure that you've been listening to everything I've said. Ask me a sensible question.

'Please, Miss. Do I have to wear my uniform when the Queen's in school?'

TEN: WATCH THAT FOOT!

The first day of a ROFTOT inspection can make everyone feel a little nervous. Even so, the day went well for the grey faced teachers at Hoddle Street. Wonderful work was going on in classrooms throughout the school; and Year 6 monitors, above all, rose to the occasion, happily fetching and carrying the seemingly endless piles of exercise books and folders which the visitors wanted to look at.

The day hadn't gone quite so well for Alan. It was, therefore, with a sense of relief that he climbed into his car. He felt tired and somewhat worried. Had the inspectors liked his sense of humour? Somehow he didn't think so. He thought back to that awkward moment in the corridor. Much of his day had been spent tramping up and down the corridors showing the ROFTOT visitors to classrooms. He flushed with embarrassment remembering how stern Mrs Piper, the Chief Inspector, had looked when he jokingly remarked that he had been 1m 86cm at the beginning of school and only 1m 60cm when the end of day bell sounded.

Another, and possibly more awkward, problem had been lurking in the back of his mind all day. How on earth could he make sure that Mavis never got to hear about his slipper? Ever since that dreadful moment just before school started he had not been able to get the thought out of his mind. As soon as he got home, he would have to dash straight upstairs and put the slipper back where it belonged – underneath the bed. That way he would not have to tell Mavis anything at all.

Shuddering slightly his thoughts went back to the morning. Early out of bed and quick off the mark, he had got to school in no time at all. The pity was that the way events unfolded he had not been able to go straight to his own office. He felt sure that everything would have been okay had he been able to go directly to his room to drink a cup of tea in the way he had planned. In the peace of the office he would have recognised immediately that something was wrong. He sighed and remembered the terrible sight. Never again would he go to work wearing one black shoe and a woolly size seven.

In his heart of hearts, he partly blamed Ms Granger for this misfortune. Without her flagpole, he was absolutely convinced things would not have been too bad. Who would have thought that Ms Granger would already have been in school? And what was the point of that flag? The last thing he had ever wanted to do at 6.45 on a dull, blustery morning was stand outside an empty school pulling hard on a rope to raise a monster of a flag which wasn't even eye catching. If it had to be a flag, it could at least have been a Union Jack or even a cross of St George. Flags, he felt sure, should be full of colour not words. *HODDLE STREET IS ON THE WAY UP AND UP* might sound impressive but surely ROFTOT inspectors were more interested in good work in classrooms!

He drove on, trying his best to remember all the jobs he had done wearing one black shoe and one woolly slipper. The day's first task had been to show the ROFTOT inspectors the way to the old Cookery room which was to be their private base throughout the week. He shuddered remembering how broadly he had smiled and how eagerly he had shaken hands. Next he had written the week's notices on the staffroom board. Finally, and perhaps worst of all, he had chatted away to Mrs Piper in his own office. The Chief Inspector had seemed friendly enough, sitting there tapping information into a lap top computer. But something about her dark green eyes and that frown had worried him. She would, he felt sure, miss very little indeed. Had she noticed the slipper?

To crown it all, Mavis had promised to be home early! For more than fifteen years, ever since training as a barrister, she had always been in court or up at her office in Banchester until mid evening. The only day she came home early was Friday when she cooked tea. But what had been her last words on this of all days? 'You've got a lot on this week, love. I'll do all the cooking. See you around 6?'

WATCH THAT FOOT!

Only one thing mattered now. Could he sneak upstairs and put the slipper back under the bed without Mavis noticing? It wouldn't be easy. The stairway in the cottage always creaked like a shipwreck. But if he managed to sneak to the top of the stairs all would be plain sailing. He tried to picture himself whistling casually, tip toeing down the stairs and strolling into the kitchen as Mavis grilled a tasty lamb chop. Yes, perhaps all would work out well.

But even in the kitchen he would have to be very careful! Under the circumstances it would be wise to avoid all conversation about the inspectors. Far better to talk about something really interesting like next Saturday's Year 6 game down at Bridley Town. And if conversation started to slacken he could talk about football training. He had been delighted to see the unlikely combination of Balraj Singh and the spindly legged Bernard Finlay turning up once again for today's after school club. Both newcomers were keen and Balraj had some skill. Mavis would no doubt be fascinated to hear that he had decided to add them to the squad for next Saturday's sizzler.

Peace reigned in Primrose Cottage. Mavis was working busily. Home early, with shopping bag in hand, she had gone straight into the kitchen and after tuning the radio in to Classical 40125, she had started to prepare a ham salad.

Mavis was also worrying. ROFTOT inspection didn't exactly sound like fun and deep down she had been worrying about her husband for some time. On the surface, he appeared to be over his disappointment. Even so, she still couldn't understand why Hoddle Street's Governors had chosen a 29 year old who didn't seem to like children as the new Headteacher. Alan had set his heart on that job.

To make matters worse, her own career was going so well. These days she could barely remember what had made her leave her part time job at the Post Office to train as a lawyer. Had she become tired of her husband's football-filled conversations? Or was it simply that she wanted to prove something to herself when Gary started school and she gained a little more time? In truth she couldn't quite remember, although she vaguely recalled that goalposts in the back garden had something to do with it.

Yes, she had never looked back since starting her second career and the whole family had gained so much from her work. It was, after all, her own high earnings which paid for their move out of Bridley to Primrose Cottage. Equally, it was her money which had financed the coaching which was now helping their younger daughter, Susan, to build a career in professional tennis.

Mavis listened carefully until she heard the car tyres splash through the puddles outside the cottage. Keen to be as helpful as possible, she was already standing in the hallway when the front door opened. Without a second's hesitation, she gave out rest-generating orders:

'Go and put your feet up whilst I fetch your slippers.'

'Don't get a drink, I'm bringing you a cup of tea.'

'Don't eat anything yet. I'm cooking you a lovely meal.'

Totally taken by surprise, Alan had no choice but to obey. Sheepishly he went into the lounge. Within a few minutes of turning on the radio and picking up the paper, he fell fast asleep on the settee.

Out in the kitchen Mavis was very puzzled. She had only found one slipper under their bed. She had searched high and low, but the second had proved impossible to find until she opened Alan's bag to put his marking on his desk!

The cooking was not going too well either. She had tried to look up 'how to make a ham salad' in her book of 'Modern Culinary Delights for Professional Couples' but there didn't seem to be any instructions. And when she had rung up her sister she had only laughed and offered no advice. Perhaps it would be wisest to nip out and buy a pizza.

ELEVEN: THE CUPBOARDS INSPECTOR

6.30 a.m. and the first to get to school, thought Alan, as he turned into the school grounds. He parked and took a final look at the checklist Mavis had written to help him. For once he felt confident: he was so well prepared that nothing could go wrong. Taking his pen from his pocket, he happily ticked off each item in turn.

Bag full of marked exercise books
Lesson plans
Tie
Best suit
And .... Shoes on both feet!

But the second he stepped out of his car into the porridge-thick gloom of the early morning, he started to lose his confidence.

From somewhere behind him he was surprised by an aggressive, though slightly squeaky, voice. 'At last! You must be the Deputy. I've been waiting here for ages wondering when on earth you'd turn up.' Startled, Alan peered through the gloom until his eyes settled on an expensive looking People Carrier in the corner of the car park.

The voice approached and Alan was able for the first time to confirm that it belonged to a physical body. From somewhere over his head it thrust out a hairy hand. Keen to impress, Alan reached up and shook firmly.

The voice squeaked again. 'I'm Hector Potts and I'm here to check your resources. I've had a word with your school keeper already and he says that most of the smaller cupboards have been left open. You'll need, of course, to get me the keys for the walk-in cupboards and show me where you keep your computers.'

Once they were inside the main building, Alan started to show the newcomer down to the old cookery room where the inspectors were leaving their bags and coats. But Hector Potts, who seemed to be in a hurry, didn't think this necessary. His voice squeaked into action once more. Its aggressive tone was beginning to bother Alan. 'Look I've had a long journey and I don't want to waste any more time. Find the keys whilst I pop outside and ring my wife on my mobile. She's a real worrier and she'll want to know I got here safely.'

Alan was trying to sort out the day's first problem when Hector Potts returned. Miss Cooper had rung in to say that she had a bad cold. With no time to get a supply teacher, the deputy had already decided to teach her class all morning. But who could teach her class during the afternoon when he had his own usual music classes to teach? The problem would have to wait.

Momentarily abandoning his desk, he took the Resources Inspector down to the first classroom, proudly showing all the beautiful new wall displays in the corridors, and pointing out that the school had recently been equipped with the latest computers. For once Hector Potts failed to squeak. Instead a much deeper grunt seemed to signal that he was suitably impressed.

Another, more personal, concern took Alan's attention. He was feeling exceptionally hungry. Somehow he had forgotten to eat his breakfast and now he was paying the price. His stomach grumbled noisily. Happily he remembered that Mavis had very kindly offered to make his lunchtime sandwiches during this very special week. Unable to resist the temptation, he opened his sandwich box and helped himself to an inviting cheese and pickle roll.

But before he could take his first bite there was a timid knock on the door. Belinda Pollard from 3T was outside. Anxious, she began breathlessly explaining that 'some grown-ups from ROFTOT' were looking at all her schoolbooks. As soon as she caught her breath, she asked her favour directly. 'Please, Sir, the visitors want my music folder. But I gave it in last lesson, sir. Can you get it from the Music Hut?'

Her request came at just the right moment and reminded the Deputy that he had far more important things to think about than his tummy. On Tuesdays, when Mrs Green taught Music over at Pixy Infants and Early Learning Centre, he always played the piano for assembly. How on earth had he managed to forget in this of all weeks? For this morning's assembly he would need a song book and the word sheets for the overhead projector. Scared that he might not be ready in time, he stepped into overdrive. His short legs crossed the playground and reached the Music Hut.

Much to his surprise, he found that Hector Potts was inside the hut. The visitor was busily writing notes on his pad and looked as grumpy as an ostrich stuck in a phone box queue. A series of squeaks did not disguise his hostility. 'What's going on? Your school keeper hasn't opened your storage room in here and you didn't even bother to give me the key. What are you hiding? My valuable time's being wasted.'

The needlessly aggressive tone began to irritate Alan. Anxious to stay cool, Alan started to explain that, apart from himself, only Mrs Green had a key to the door. Unfortunately, Hector Potts no longer seemed interested in hearing what he had to say.

More and more frustrated, the Deputy took out the large bunch of jangling keys which weighed down his jacket so much. Opening the storage room door abruptly, he grabbed Belinda's folder, snatched the overhead word sheets and grabbed a song book. With almost exaggerated friendliness, he invited the aggressive squeaker to take a much closer look inside. 'Thank goodness there's plenty in there to keep him busy until assembly's finished,' he said to himself as he hurried back to the main building.

The varying sounds of a short tape of classical music – one moment Brahms and the next Beethoven – filled the air as classes gathered in the hall. Looking for all the world like someone trapped on a sandbank as high tide approaches, Alan directed each class to its position. Year 3 always sat closest to the stage; knowing the daily routine so well now, they glided silently to their places with the effortless ease of a puck on ice. Once everyone had settled, a secret nod to Jenny Khan, the assembly monitor, produced action. She slipped out of the back of the hall to let Ms Granger know that everything was ready. Alan took up his place on the piano stool ready to play the first song.

The assembly did not go well. Under normal circumstances, even when sitting at the upright piano, Alan could hear everything Ms Granger said. But this morning was different. Far less confident than normal, the Head spoke in a voice which was barely more than a whisper. To make matters worse, the central heating system had been set on maximum and with the hall hot, crowded and airless it proved hard to stay awake.

Ms Granger droned on ever more drearily, like an out of breath bagpipe not quite able to reach the end of a slow march.

All too quickly, the early start to the day, the heat, and the Head's dull voice worked their magic. Last night, in order to be perfectly prepared for his day, Alan had worked until the early hours. Then, once in bed he had tossed and turned, dreaming about ROFTOT inspectors. And now, at precisely the wrong moment, sleep had arrived!

Desperate to stay awake, the Deputy took action. He pinched his legs sharply and then, taking advantage of his hidden position behind the piano, he started to look around. Why did the hall seem so crowded this morning? All the classes were sitting in their usual places..... Glancing further he was utterly taken aback. There were 5,6,7,8....9 inspectors in the hall.

His eyes next settled on Year 3 and for the first time he noticed that many of the smallest children were also sleepy. The whole of Row 1 were in obvious difficulty. Little heads were bobbing up and down like chickens pecking for grain as they struggled to stay awake.

And then the silence of the hall was disturbed by that most distinctive of sounds.

S....nore, S.........nore, S.........NORE

For a moment the Deputy kept his head down and struggled not to giggle. When at long last he felt able to look up, his worst suspicions were confirmed. There, right in the middle of the second row, with eyes tight shut, Belinda Pollard was snoring. Her angelic face misled. She sounded like a sergeant major with a sinus problem. The inspectors must have noticed! With heads dipped low, they wrote fast and furiously like secretaries employed by ambitious politicians.

Ms Granger remained on the stage long after the final class had left the hall. She seemed a little distracted and Alan was reluctant to disturb her. Instead, he set about the usual end of assembly tasks. First he put the overhead projector away for its well earned rest. Then he thanked the ever reliable monitors from 6V who always seemed to sense the exact numbers of chairs needed for grown ups in the hall. 'Excellent! You did well to find chairs for all those visitors,' he remarked cheerfully as they trundled off to class.

Turning around he noticed that Ms Granger was still on the stage. She was undoubtedly upset and her words of advice at the last staff meeting before the visitors arrived came into his mind. 'We must stick together at all costs during ROFTOT week,' she had advised, smiling broadly and revealing a mouthful of dental perfection.

For a moment the Deputy scratched the top of his head and tried to decide what to say. But even before he had finished thinking he found that his tongue was already moving: 'I enjoyed this morning's assembly, Ms Granger. Good idea to make it so boring. Lots of Year 3 were very sleepy when they went back to class. I'm sure they'll all work quietly in today's lessons.'

Unfortunately, Ms Granger did not like his comment. From up on the stage, perched on the high heels which made her seem taller than ever, she glared at him. Her spectacles slipped a full centimetre down her nose giving her sometimes fox-like face a strange bird-like quality. Her tongue took flight. 'I thought you said you were going to cover Miss Cooper's class,' she reminded him sharply, using a voice cold enough to freeze freshly boiled water.

Under the circumstances, Alan was glad to escape to a classroom. Much to his relief he found that Miss Cooper had left detailed plans for her Numeracy Hour. He always liked 3T and his time with the group would no doubt be enjoyable. He read her instructions again ….. Mental Maths and continuation of work on tessellation …. workbooks in cupboard. Workbooks in cupboard? No problem! He went over to the cupboard door. Locked ? Shouldn't be, with the Resources Inspector in school.

He reached into his pocket for his master keys.

Not there. Where could they be?

He tried to think where he had been and realised almost at once that he must have left the keys over in the Music Hut. Quickly, taking advantage of the presence of the kindly Mrs Khan, the support assistant who did such excellent work with 3T, Alan slipped out of the classroom.

Inside the Music Hut, he found the keys exactly where he had left them in the open door of the storage room. Alan grabbed the keys. Anxious by now that the class might be getting a little noisy, he paused only to lock the main door leading into the hut and sped back to class.

He need not have worried. The class were enjoying their investigation and a pleasant bubble of constructive discussion even made him feel sorry that no inspector was watching!

After morning break things did not go quite so well. Literacy Hour had hardly begun when Sally gave a message via the school's loud speaker system. Even her smooth secretarial tones could not disguise her obvious concern: 'Mr Ramsbottom, Ms Granger needs you urgently in the Administration Block.' Red as an overripe tomato, Alan handed over to Mrs Khan, and rushed from the room for a second time.

When he reached the Administration Block, he found that the school office was in chaos. The school nurse, Mrs Maudsley, was waving her arms and saying, 'I bet he's been kidnapped.' Fortunately, the unflappable Sally was much calmer. She beckoned Alan over and whispered in his ear. 'Look, we've got a real problem. One of the inspectors should have seen Ms Granger after assembly but he seems to have vanished into thin air.'

'Which one?' asked Alan. 'Not that awkward chap who wants to look in all the cupboards, I hope.'

'You've got it in one,' said Sally, looking at him rather curiously. 'How on earth did you guess that? Actually, we've already checked all the walk-in cupboards in case he fainted or something but we've not found him anywhere.'

Alan digested this information before asking the important question:

'Look, are we sure we've really checked everywhere?'

'Of course,' snapped Sally with uncharacteristic irritation.

'Including that old P.E. storage room that the lads re-discovered the other day?'

'Of course,' shouted Sally, almost losing her cool.

Alan shuffled his feet and desperately tried to think.

'What about the one over in the Music Hut?' he started to say slowly.

Without waiting for her reply, he leapt into action. As he raced across the playground, he heard muffled cries and recognised the angry face peering through the hut window.

The shouting stopped as Alan turned the key. For a moment there was silence. Then, almost flattening the Deputy as he pushed the door open, Hector Potts charged out onto the playground.

TWELVE: IS MS GRANGER ANGRY?

Wednesday began mistily. A cold, grey band gripped the fields tightly like a dog collar round a curate's neck. The mist made the short journey down the twisting lanes to Bridley hazardous and demanded full attention.

Alan was fretting. All night long he had tossed and turned, wondering whether the Head would find some way to punish him because of the great 'Resources Inspector locked in a Music Hut' fiasco.

It would all, of course, have been so much easier had he been able to apologise at the right time. But Hector Potts had moved far too quickly for that. Like an angry rhino charging across a great African plain, he had stormed over to Ms Granger's office the second he was free. Anxious to say sorry, Alan had followed. But a notice saying *'Do not disturb under any circumstances'* immediately appeared on the Headteacher's door. With communication impossible, Alan had gone off to teach without knowing what had been said. All the Deputy knew was what Sally had told him at the end of the day. Hector Potts had last been seen driving out of the school gates at high speed.

Alan started work. Hands shaking, he began to put the day's notices on the staffroom board.

As he concentrated, he suddenly felt a firm grip on his shoulder. Startled he jumped and turned around. Much to his relief, it was Leroy Jones, his best friend on the staff. Leroy looked serious and said, 'Look man, I've got a problem. The History Inspector's stuck in my classroom but I can't find the key. Can you help?' For a moment, Alan went as red as a six year old caught with a hand in a biscuit tin. But then they both laughed. 'Just stay cool, man, and have a nice day,' added Leroy, leaving with a friendly wave.

Feeling more relaxed now, Alan continued his task: Miss Cooper duty in playground; Mrs Hussain to corridor 2; Miss Muriel Jones to dining hall.

Again, he felt a gentle tap on his shoulder. 'Look, pack it in, Leroy. Don't you know when a joke's over,' grumbled Alan, completing a 180 degree turn. He instantly recognised his mistake. Leroy was nowhere to be seen. Instead, in front of him was a small, young, grey suited woman. Large pink ear rings dangled below her small pink ears like champion conkers on strings. Ears and ear rings matched perfectly the pink-cased lap top computer clutched tightly by nail varnished fingers. The badge on the newcomer's jacket read: Ms Millicent Bourne Cosin, Inspector for Special Needs.

For the second time in less than five minutes, Alan turned tomato red. But Ms Bourne Cosin's twinkling eyes suggested amusement not anger. 'Don't worry! Everybody's always over excited when ROFTOT are around,' she said brightly as Alan took her to collect the pupil folders she needed from the locked filing cabinets in the Administration Block.

Life had begun to get better by the time first lesson started. Alan always looked forward to his lesson with 5T, his favourite class in the Upper School. All week he had been hoping that someone from ROFTOT would drop in to see him teach this lesson. They would see his best work here, he felt sure.

On Wednesdays, when Mrs Green taught in the Music Hut all day, he used the Drama Studio for his own music classes. The room was far from perfect but at least it gave everyone a good chance to spread out for group work. The one problem was the piano. It had lots of missing notes and a honky tonk tone suitable only for the saloon scene in a cowboy film.

Whenever he worked in the Drama Studio, Alan managed without the piano, relying instead on an assortment of instruments borrowed from the Music Hut. This was only made possible through the efforts of Josh, Mandy, Fahim and Abigail, the team of eager monitors from 5T. Every Wednesday they missed assembly, spending their time heading to and from the Music Hut, overloaded with triangles, tin whistles, drums and chime bars.

Would one of the ROFTOT inspectors drop in to watch this lesson? Always full of life, 5T knew how to have fun whilst working hard. Well before Miss Phelps brought her class down to the Drama Studio, the Deputy was ready and waiting, eager for action. The children filed in quietly, helping themselves to chairs and forming a semi circle. Alan smiled broadly, offering congratulations for a quiet arrival.

He was just about to begin when there was a purposeful knock. In walked a short, bearded, grey-haired, clipboard-carrying inspector. The ROFTOT representative made his way to the back of the room leaving a trail of after shave in his wake. For a moment Alan lost his concentration. 'Why does a bearded inspector smell so strongly of after shave?' he wondered, silently mystified.

For a second time, Alan tried to start. He smiled brightly and said, 'I think we'll have a great lesson today 5T. The aim of our lesson will be to............' Like a car engine running out of fuel, his voice ground to a halt. Another loud knock on the studio door signalled that he was to be interrupted once again.

The class were amused, but before anybody could leap off their chairs, Alan opened the door. Outside stood Ms Granger. Fixing him tightly in her gaze, she glared over the top of her gold rimmed reading glasses. A full half minute must have passed before she said anything. Usually she spoke quite quickly. Yet she chose to use the very slow voice which elderly teachers who have taught infants for all of their working lives use by instinct. Since she was under thirty and perfectly capable of speaking at a normal speed her intention was clear.

'Good morning, Alan. I am so sorry that I must disturb you. I hope that no ROFTOT representative is with you at the moment,' said Ms Granger with all the speed of a tortoise crossing the Sahara Desert. As she continued, there were telltale signs that 5T were becoming restless. Chime bars chimed, shakers rattled and somewhere in the background Alan heard the low, almost volcanic, sound of the big bass drum.

IS MS GRANGER ANGRY?

Speaking ever more slowly, like a clockwork toy which needed re-winding, Ms Granger finally reached her point. 'I want you to meet Parminder and Pritti, Alan. They're twins and they're joining us today. I've put them in 5T.' Pritti and Parminder smiled, saying nothing.

Shuffling feet, tapping hands, and the shaking, pulling, blowing and pushing of assorted instruments created a wall of sound as Alan stepped back into the Drama Studio. Warmly welcoming the newcomers, he made a determined effort to re-start.

This time his best efforts were upset by the bearded inspector. For at precisely this moment the visitor rubbed his beard. Immediately this seemed to release more after shave into the atmosphere. Half the class began to cough and splutter. Totally unaware of the consequences of his action, the inspector yawned, stretched his arms and started to write on his notepad.

Again Alan tried to start the lesson. He put a cassette in the recorder and paused as if expecting another tap on the door. No sound came. Happy at last, he turned on the tape. A jolly sing-along voice began a jolly sing-along song: 'Good morning, Teacher, good morning, children. Welcome to our fifth programme in our 'Sounds from the 60s' series'.

Even before the sing-along voice had completed its jolly sing-along introduction, someone knocked on the door.

This time Ms Granger marched straight in. And this time she was almost hidden in a crowd. For a group of casually dressed students marched in behind her. Most of the young men had single ear rings and closely cropped hair or pony tails. In contrast, the women appeared to be identically dressed in long multi coloured cardigans and flared trousers.

'I know you won't have forgotten that we have fourteen trainee social workers from European countries with us this morning,' said Ms Granger. 'They're a little late, but I know that you will be keen that they should have a chance to see you teach Music.'

'So kind, Headteacher,' gasped Alan weakly. 'So kind.' But what on earth could he do?

Strangely, as if sensing that Ms Granger was trying to be

awkward, 5T took charge.

'Would you like us to give a concert of all the songs we've been learning?' someone helpfully suggested.

'Great idea,' gasped Alan, like a dying goldfish fighting for its last breath.

The class took over. In no time at all they created a rhythm section and worked their way through five songs earning a burst of tumultuous applause from the trainee social workers who were all sitting down cross legged by the side of the bearded inspector.

There were, however, still five minutes left. What could be done to fill the time? Anxiously Alan picked up a tabla drum and asked whether anyone could play it. Much to his surprise, the first hands to shoot into the air were those of Parminder and Pritti.

'I play the tabla really well, man,' exclaimed Parminder, 'and, if you like, my sister will play the sitar.'

'Wonderful,' spluttered Alan, inviting them to the front.

With grace, dexterity and almost perfect timing the twins played a series of haunting melodies. Pritti's delicate finger work produced a soft yet rich sound from the sitar which contrasted wonderfully with her brother's firm rhythmic tapping on the tabla drum.

Everyone listened, entranced. Then, finally, as the last note sounded, the class burst into applause. For a moment the cross legged social workers remained on the floor. However, suddenly realising that the music had indeed finished, they too leapt to their feet shouting, 'Bravo! Bravo! More! More!'

Only the short, bearded and heavily after-shaved inspector seemed unmoved. His short, mysterious figure remained rooted to its back corner seat until all the children had filed out of the Drama Studio. But then the pungent smell of after shave moved ever closer as he crossed the room to speak to Alan. 'Not a bad lesson, not a bad lesson,' he whispered.

The Deputy smiled weakly and struggled not to cough.

THIRTEEN: LOOK BEFORE YOU LEG IT

Stars were shining across the clear, mid-evening sky when Mavis arrived home from Banchester. As usual, she parked her car in the driveway outside the garage. So hungry that she might even enjoy the mushroom and sprout soup Alan had promised for supper, she took no interest in the heavens. Instead, gathering her bags, and pausing only to make sure that no dogs were lurking behind the rhododendrons, she hurried to the door.

To her surprise, Bill Prentice, the local bobby, was on the door step. Now close to retirement, he had known Mavis for years.

'Glad to see you, young lady,' he said brightly. 'Been leaning on doorbell for ages but can't wake up that husband of yours. Couldn't get hold of Ms Granger neither. He's needed down at police station. Chief Superintendent's wanting me back like half an hour ago.'

'Oh goodness,' muttered Mavis. 'Not another break-in at school, I hope.'

' 'Fraid so,' replied Bill, ' but at least we seem to have the blighter.'

It was clear that Bill was anxious not to waste more time. Unfortunately, Mavis couldn't find her key. With the policeman watching closely, she felt embarrassed. She began to pull things out of her sheepskin handbag: lip stick, eye shadow, glasses case, dental floss, contact lens cleaner, handkerchief. Eventually, the bag seemed reasonably empty. But no key had emerged. With an air of desperation, Mavis held the bag upside down. Out tumbled her barrister's wig. It landed on the doorstep with a dull clink, like a lonely coin dropping into an empty charity box.

Mavis viewed the wig suspiciously as if half expecting it to scurry away into the rhododendrons. Cautiously using the end of her umbrella, she picked it up and removed a large brass key. 'It's got a life of its own, that wig,' she mumbled. Then, remembering her visitor, she added more loudly, 'It's here. Nice and safe. Just where I like to keep it.'

Mavis turned the key. Unfortunately, the door failed to open because Alan had bolted it from inside.

'Brave men first,' she suggested playfully, waiting for her solid companion to do his duty. 'Been hoping you'd say that, young 'un,' said Bill playfully. Using his full weight, the constable pushed hard. The whole frame shook until the reluctant door gave up its resistance.

Looking very pleased with himself, the brave and bulky constable wiped sturdy size 14 shoes on the doormat. A loud and unmistakable sound of snoring filled the hallway. It was coming from the lounge. Mud trailed across polished tiles as, like an elephant making a guest appearance for the royal ballet, Bill tried to tiptoe into the room.

Peeping around the door, suspicions were confirmed. There, on the settee, Alan was fast asleep.

Keen to keep the constable waiting no longer than necessary, Mavis tapped her husband's shoulder and whispered something into his ear. This did the trick. After a moment or two he woke up. Stretching arms and rubbing his eyes, he sat up straight. He was obviously puzzled to see Bill Prentice. 'Good to see you, officer,' he said, voice rising in curiosity.

An offer of a lift to the police station was immediately accepted. Putting on his seat belt, Alan was amused to find that nosy neighbours were watching from behind half closed curtains. 'Shall I put on the siren and blue light?' joked Bill, reversing quickly out of the driveway.

Down at the station Alan was hurried into the heart of the building without even checking in with the desk sergeant. He followed the constable along dismal corridors until they reached a large waiting room. 'I'll pop and see if Chief's ready' said Bill.

Though freshly painted, the room housed few objects of interest. A tired looking rubber plant, three rows of cheap plastic chairs and a large 'No Smoking' sign all failed to hold attention. The sound of bubbling drew Alan's eyes towards a tank of tropical fish. As if tragically cut off from his oxygen supply, a model diver lay helplessly on his side in the bottom of the tank. Beneath a single fluorescent light a small shoal of guppies swam in close formation like an airforce display team at a summer show.

The waiting room was almost empty. Its only occupants were an Asian mother, her adult son and three toddlers who were possibly grand children. Dressed in a green sari and wearing a traditional headscarf, the mother was reading an English cookery magazine. The adult son was enormous. As big as any American wrestler, he was casually dressed in a track suit. His broad shoulders were bouncing up and down as he listened to a headset. The toddlers were alternating their attention between the fish tank and the contents of a box of toys. Alan suddenly noticed that Balraj Singh was the final member of the group.

Upon Alan's arrival, the adult son levered himself off the seats. Stepping slowly forward, he suddenly spoke with the speed of an express train. 'Alright, sir. Remember me? Used to be in your class seven years ago.'

The Deputy gave the impression that he remembered. Somewhat cautiously he put out his right hand. The young man took it, hid it momentarily inside his own huge fist, and crushed tightly. With a look which suggested that he should have known better, Alan reclaimed his hand.

Balraj joined the welcoming party. 'Nice to see you, sir. Met my cousin Hardeep before?' he asked innocently. But before Alan could reply, Bill Prentice returned. 'Chief's ready,' said the constable, before knocking on a door labelled 'Detective Chief Superintendent.' A confident voice shouted 'Enter'.

The Chief Superintendent's room had a high ceiling, but was in all other ways very small indeed. Nobody was sitting on the large swivel chair behind the large oak desk which filled half the room. For the second time in a matter of seconds, Alan was puzzled. Where had the voice come from?

'47, 48' sang the voice from somewhere near his feet. The Deputy peeped under the table.

'49, 50' said the voice, completing her sit-ups and flopping onto the swivel chair.

Alan took a closer look. He seemed to recognise the face.

'Haven't I seen you somewhere before?' he asked uncertainly.

'Yes, much earlier today, don't you remember,' replied the Chief Superintendent. 'Can I give you a clue? When we met you were writing on a notice board.'

The Deputy rubbed his still tired eyes and looked at the Chief Inspector with new curiosity. Where had he seen the face before? Then it came to him. This had to be Millicent Bourne Cosin. 'You're not really a schools inspector, then?' he asked faintly.

'Oh, no' giggled Chief Superintendent Bourne Cosin. 'I'm a detective. I was just down at Hoddle Street in the course of duty following a tip off. 'I enjoyed my bit of acting but the person I was after didn't turn up.' She paused as if keen to allow this information to sink in. 'Doesn't matter now, though,because tonight we've got our man.'

Smiling broadly, the detective jumped off her swivel chair. 'Come and take a look through here.' Squeezing through the small gap behind her chair, she stretched upwards on tip toes and opened a small cupboard door to reveal a two way mirror. 'Look through there. Do you know him?' she whispered softly.

Alan peered through. The light in the interview room was poor. But every few seconds the unreliable fluorescent light flickered and kicked back fully into life. He peered more closely. There, slumped forward on the chair, with his head in his hands, was the unmistakable figure of Hector Potts.

'But he's a Cupboards Inspector!' said Alan.

'Oh no he isn't, Oh no he *ain't*,' replied Millicent, emphasising her *ain't* with obvious pleasure. She chuckled and danced a jolly little 'Dosy Doe' around the increasingly puzzled Deputy. 'Follow me and meet my helpers.'

She opened a door. To his surprise, Alan found himself back in the waiting room. 'The heroes of the hour,' said Millicent, leading him over to Balraj and his family.

Catching Hector Potts was, as Balraj proudly explained, 'quite easy'. Along with his huge cousin, he had been playing cricket in his uncle's back garden until, unimpressed by Balraj's feeble 'fast' bowling, Hardeep had struck a mighty blow.

The house backed onto Hoddle Street's playing field and the shot launched the ball skyward like a rocket leaving a launch pad. Eventually gravity won the battle and it returned to earth having cleared the whole school building!

Feeling rather guilty that he had lost his little cousin's tennis ball, Hardeep had decided to find it straight away. He was unable to squeeze his sumo wrestler-like figure through the small break in their garden fence and so the pair had gone to the school's main entrance.

Their search had at first been unsuccessful. Soon they realised that this was not merely because it was almost completely dark. As the moon started to rise in the sky, it became clear that someone had been digging in the grass quadrangle between the main building and the Administration Block.

Still getting to know the school, Balraj had vaguely remembered Ms Granger warning everyone 'to keep away from the holes on the grass'. That very morning in assembly she had told them all to have a good look at the giant new *'Hoddle Street is on its way up and up'* flag outside the Administration Block.

But what had she added? Her words, he felt sure, had been a warning.

'Keep off the grass between the main building and the Administration Block.'

What else had she said?

'Bridley Council have now finished digging all of the holes ready for flags from many parts of the world. They will look superb when the Mayor comes for the official opening of the Administration Block. SO KEEP OFF THE GRASS.'

The pair looked into sixteen holes and then found the ball. Unfortunately, their triumph turned out to be short-lived. For at precisely that moment a burglar alarm sounded. Within seconds, a tall shadowy figure stumbled out of the new offices struggling under the weight of a new computer.

Taking giant ostrich-like strides, he cut across the grass towards the car park. This was a mistake. For almost immediately he lost his footing, tripped and tumbled headfirst into a particularly large flagpole hole.

Boy and young man looked on in utter amazement. Hector Potts' ankles were stuck in two of the smaller holes whilst his upper body had disappeared into a larger moonlike crater.

With surprising speed for a big man, Hardeep put his own rugby playing skills to good effect. Like a giant second row forward keen to catch up with a loose scrum, he charged over to the sprawled figure. Then, flopping on top of him, he allowed the would-be burglar to feel the full force of his 19 stones.

Within moments the police had arrived.

FOURTEEN: INSPECTORS HAVE THEIR SAY

The best assemblies were always on Fridays! Most other days senior teachers still read from a thick and well thumbed volume called 'A hundred and one last minute assemblies'. But, much to her credit, Ms Granger was trying to improve things. She had nicknamed the book 'Assemblies heard a hundred and one times before' and had introduced special class assemblies on the last day of each week. These assemblies, which each class planned in turn, were always interesting and entertaining.

Today's assembly would be from 6Q. Somehow the idea of a 6Q assembly made Alan uneasy. Would someone say something silly? Or would it simply be a Mrs Witherspoon special – long-winded and boring?

The one good thing was that *all* the inspectors had finished their work! Only Mrs Piper was still around and she was over in Ms Granger's office. At this very moment the Chief ROFTOT Inspector would no doubt be explaining what the visitors would write in their report about Hoddle Street. So far as Alan knew, even Mrs Piper would be gone by 10 a.m. The Chief Inspector had already explained that she would leave long before the Mayor of Bridley arrived for the grand opening of the Administration Block.

Feeling very relieved that nobody from ROFTOT was in the assembly hall, the Deputy handed over to 6Q who had just arrived from their last minute practice in the Drama Studio. He made way for the Lewis twins. Their job was to check that all their classmates were kneeling or sitting in the correct place until their turn to speak. When everyone had settled they nodded to Marcus, who was clearly going to be the first to say something, and he stepped confidently out into the centre of the stage. Next they signalled to Balraj and Bernard, who were crouching down, evidently in the wrong positions, at the edge of the stage. Rather sheepishly they clambered over a number of classmates and joined their friend.

Not at all put off by this minor mishap, Marcus stayed cool.
'Good morning, Mr Ramsbottom

Good morning, teachers.

Good morning everybody.

Oh, and I almost forgot to say, *good morning inspector sitting quietly in the corner.*'

Looking up from his chair, Alan was utterly dismayed. For there, sitting quietly at the back of the hall was the short, bearded, heavily after-shaved inspector. What was going on? Hadn't the inspectors left?

'Welcome to 6Q's assembly,' said Balraj, grinning from ear to ear.

'We hope our assembly will make you think,' added Bernard, reading slowly from a card gripped tightly in shaking hands.

Within seconds four classmates appeared. They trundled onto the stage carrying a card table. The Lewis twins followed carrying six biscuit tins. Each tin was different:

One was old....... One was new

One was black.....One was white

One was big........One was small

Next on stage was Charmaine Bradley, the star striker from the Year 6 football team, who for once in her life was not kicking a football. Using a remarkably grown up voice, she asked whether anyone would like a biscuit. 'We would like biscuits,' chorused six classmates from somewhere behind the piano. In a short crocodile they swaggered onto the stage. Without looking, they eagerly plunged their hands into the biscuit barrels. By the time they returned to their hiding place biscuits had been taken from each tin.

Within seconds, Marcus re-appeared. Now wearing a clergyman's dog collar (a shirt turned round backwards) he looked very happy with life. He grinned broadly and put on a powerful voice like an American preacher posing a soul searching question.

'Can anyone tell me the lesson of today's assembly?'
He pointed to a Year 3 pupil:
'Eat biscuits for breakfast,' she whispered uncertainly.
He pointed to someone from Year 4:
'Biscuits are usually kept in tins,' he suggested after scratching his head.
He pointed in the direction of a girl in Year 5:
'You can always find a biscuit if you look hard enough,' she replied, causing all her friends to giggle.

Throughout the hall there were signs of unrest as giggles broke out like a Mexican wave. But immediately Marcus took command. 'No, no, no,' roared Marcus, his voice rising like a preacher with a congregation in the palm of his hand. 'Can all of 6Q join me on the stage again, please?'

The whole class trooped back onto the stage, some nervously, some obviously embarrassed, others brimming with confidence. 'I hope you all got the point of our assembly,' said Marcus. In pairs, his classmates raised a series of posters.

DON'T JUDGE FROM THE OUTSIDE
IT'S WHAT WE'RE LIKE ON THE INSIDE WHICH COUNTS
WE ARE ALL DIFFERENT AND WE ARE ALL THE SAME

For a moment Marcus paused. Then, like a preacher unsure when the moment to stop speaking had arrived, he carried on. ' I hope you noticed that all the tins looked different. But inside they were all the same. They all contained biscuits. ....

But nobody heard his next word! For a sudden commotion at the back of the hall brought his explanation to a halt. Shouting 'Bravo', the short, bearded and heavily after-shaved inspector had leapt to his feet. This caused great confusion and an outbreak of coughing. ' Bravo, splendid,' he shouted again and again, and from all around the hall there was thunderous applause as row after row of children started to clap.

Assembly now over, Mrs Green played the piano softly as each class filed out of the hall. Then, picking up her music and hurrying off to teach, she left the Deputy alone in the hall with nothing to do but put away the overhead projector and close the piano lid.

Several windows near the back of the hall where Year 6 had been sitting were open and Alan moved over to close them. But as he did so he suddenly became acutely aware of the smell of after shave. Turning around sharply, he discovered that he was not alone.

The short, bearded, heavily after-shaved inspector was the first to break the silence. 'After seeing that great assembly I feel that I should show you something before I leave.' Stroking the end of his beard thoughtfully, the inspector left his words hanging in the air like a recently released glider. Blissfully unaware that the Deputy was beginning to wheeze, he suddenly continued. 'I'm sure by now you have guessed that I'm not really a ROFTOT inspector.' Again he paused. Then, quick as a flash, he raised his hands and pulled off his beard!

The air at once seemed clearer and Alan listened in astonishment as the visitor had his final say. 'I'm an INSPECTOR OF INSPECTORS,' said the short, heavily after-shaved clean shaven visitor, his voice rising in excitement like a newly released hot air balloon. 'I've had my suspicions about that Cupboards Inspector for quite some time. Imagine how I chuckled when I learnt that you had locked him up the other day! Imagine my delight when the police rang me last night! Well done, well done!'

When, a little later, Alan went over to the Administration Block, Victoria Piper, the Chief ROFTOT Inspector, and Ms Granger were deep in conversation. The door of the office was wide open and Ms Granger was smiling. A good sign?

Immediately noticing that the atmosphere was more relaxed than usual, Alan flopped into the easy chair which Robin Johnstone usually claimed. 'I suppose you're looking forward to getting your feet up at the end of the week, Alan,' said Mrs Piper gently. Her solemn face offered few clues. Was she still thinking of the slipper he had been wearing when they first met? Correctly sensing that she was indeed friendly now, Alan joked that he was saving his slippers until after Hoddle Street's game at Bridley Town.

'Two lumps or three, Alan?' asked Ms Granger. 'By the way, put me down to help with lifts tomorrow. I'll bring that nice man who helped out last night. What was his name? Hardeep? Didn't you say that he's an old pupil?'

With growing pride, Head and Deputy listened as Mrs Piper explained how impressed she had been by children's work around the school. But all the time Alan couldn't help wondering whether she would mention Hector Potts. The Chief ROFTOT Inspector seemed to read his mind.

'I know Ms Granger's been exploding like a volcano all week because you locked up one of my inspectors. But you didn't, did you, Alan?'

'No,' replied Alan, puzzled.

'No,' repeated Mrs Piper firmly.

'No,' responded Alan, like an uncertain parrot.

'No,' replied Mrs Piper as she stood up to leave. 'Don't worry. All you did was lock up a crook who was trying to work out what to steal. Not the same thing, is it?'

FIFTEEN: NOW THE WEEK IS OVER!

Alan listened carefully. The sound of the singing school keeper made him hurry. Every Friday, come sunshine or shadow, Tom sang the same song as he closed windows and checked that all the classroom doors were locked.

Now the day is over
Night is drawing nigh
Shadows of the evening
Flit across the sky

On Fridays, when Tom went to his sister's for tea, it was understood that everyone had to be out of the school building before 5 p.m. And on this Friday of all Fridays there should be no delay! Anxious not to keep him waiting, and aware that the singing was becoming much louder with every second, the Deputy turned off his lamp and gathered folders from his desk. Collecting a tray of exercise books from the top of his bookcase, he stepped out into the corridor and closed the door.

This was a moment they knew well. The passing of seasons and the rolling away of years never seemed to make any difference at all. On Fridays at 5 p.m. precisely Alan would lose his keys. And no scientific knowledge was needed to state with absolute certainty where Alan and Tom could always be found at 5.15. Without fail they would still be in school, down on their hands and knees searching for the missing bunch. Almost always this weekly ritual would draw to its close at 5.20 when the keys would 'miraculously' turn up where they had been all along – in the Deputy's pocket.

Feeling pleased that he had for once got out of his office before the 5 p.m. deadline, Alan plunged his hands into the depths of his jacket pockets. Sewing had never been a strong point in the Ramsbottom household and, like nervous rabbits disturbed by late evening joggers, keys were for ever disappearing down mysterious holes into the jacket's silky black lining. Once well hidden they could prove difficult to find and even harder to retrieve. For once, Alan found the keys quickly. He would be able to leave before Tom reached his door.

Unfortunately the Deputy could not get his keys out of his pocket. Tangled in cotton fibre and firmly stuck to an unwrapped and long forgotten toffee they were as firmly trapped as a fly in a spider's web. He took off his jacket, pulled hard and in great triumph successfully freed them seconds before the singing school keeper arrived.

'Locking up already, Alan? What's the world coming to?' said Tom jokingly. The Deputy also smiled and for once managed a quick reply. ' I'm just off to iron all the football shirts for tomorrow. You never know I might call you in the morning if I'm short of any players!'

It was raining steadily as Alan steered the hatchback between the puddles on the staff car park. Under a golfing umbrella, Tom was already by the school gates clutching a padlock. With a thumbs up and a smile the Deputy turned out onto the road.

The Bridley roads were always at their most congested on dismal Friday afternoons. For the first kilometre Alan automatically followed the back route, a short cut leading over humps and up and down some cobbled streets near school. Eventually he had no choice but to turn out onto the open road. Here traffic appeared to be going nowhere as, like snails edging across a damp paving stone, cars inched forward. The late afternoon gloom was punctured by the sound of irritable motorists needlessly blowing their car horns.

Alan turned on his radio to keep out unwanted noise. Tuning in to Radio Bridley, he caught the latest sports news. Lorna Massie, presenter of 'Have a Good Week End' was looking ahead to the Bridley Town v Banchester United clash. Listening intently, he felt a sudden surge of pride as he heard her claim that that much interest would centre upon how well Gary Ramsbottom played following his controversial summer transfer.

Feeling a little disappointed that no mention had been made of the other game – the great half time clash between Hoddle Street and Anniversary Lane Primary School – Alan turned off the radio. His thoughts returned to some of the main events of the day.

How wrong Robin Johnstone had been! The big news was that Mrs Piper had gone away 'reasonably impressed' by what she had seen, even though she felt more hard work was needed before Ms Granger's ambitious claim that Hoddle Street was on its way 'up and up' was completely true.

And how odd it was that flags had played such an important part in the week!

And what about 6Q ? That assembly had been brilliant. Was it their own idea? How had Mrs Witherspoon helped?

And what about Mrs Witherspoon? Was she changing? How splendidly she had come to the rescue when everything went wrong at the last moment.

His thoughts returned to the early afternoon. All those parents on the car park. Flags from around the world blowing in the breeze. Refreshments ready, red carpet unrolled. Classes gathering on the grass to witness the grand opening.

And then that strange moment in the office. Sudden panic when the Mayor's secretary came on the phone with that awful message. *'The Mayor is sorry that he is unavoidably delayed. He has to stay at the Finance Committee and he won't now be along to open your new Administration Block for another hour. I hope you will be able to keep all the parents and children happy until he arrives!'*

How lucky it was that Mrs Witherspoon had that good idea. A parents v pupils hockey match! All the mums and dads were enjoying their game so much that everybody was most disappointed when the Mayor's limousine finally pulled into the car park.

The words from that assembly were so true, he reflected. *You really should be careful not to judge by appearances.*

SIXTEEN: THE BIG MATCH

Has there ever been anywhere noisier that the inside of a junior school mini bus on the way to a football match? On a small planet in a different galaxy out on the far reaches of the known universe there may, indeed, be such a place. But Alan Ramsbottom doubted it. Tucked behind the steering wheel, heading towards the Bridley v Banchester clash and the eagerly anticipated titanic struggle between Hoddle Street and Anniversary Lane Primary, his head felt like the inside of a volcano.

Everybody had so much to say and even more to shout! Sitting in the back corner, Marcus was explaining at the top of his voice that no goals would slip through his hands. Charmaine Bradley, centre forward extraordinary, was boasting that she would slam at least three goals into the net. Even the Lewis twins were having their say. Unaware that they were very fortunate to be in the starting line-up at all, both were supremely confident that they would create match-winning overlaps from their wide positions as right and left wing backs.

Head thumping, Alan looked into his mirror and observed the open-topped sports car which was following closely. Face half hidden by her claret and green scarf, Ms Granger was chatting to Hardeep Singh.

And what of Balraj and Bernard? As newcomers, neither had made the starting line-up. Delighted to be pencilled in as 'additional substitutes', they now found themselves in the back of Mrs Witherspoon's car. At this very moment, therefore, they were a little further back in the line of stationary traffic building up on the by-pass.

There were bound to be delays before kick-off. The combination of early Christmas shoppers driving into town and Bridley supporters heading out to the new ground brought all traffic to a standstill.

How many years was it since Bridley had pulled in such a crowd? Looking in the mirror once again, Alan could see cars stretching over the Brick Works bridge and on into the distant centre of town. But why was nothing moving forward? Up ahead the worst congestion definitely seemed to be at the Bragg Road traffic lights. Everyone wanted to turn right to enter the car parks outside the ground and only three or four vehicles could make their move each time the lights turned green.

With mounting tension and a tightening chest, Alan waited. 1.45 already! At this rate they would end up late. A horrible thought crossed his mind and he imagined an article in the Bridley News.

TEAM ARRIVES TOO LATE!
Deputy Headteacher Alan Ramsbottom has apologised for all the upset he caused last Saturday. Hoddle Street Junior School had been chosen to play a short half time match against local rivals Anniversary Lane Primary School during the Bridley Banchester sizzler. Unfortunately, the dozy Deputy arrived so late that his team missed their chance ...

The arrival of a policewoman on a motor bike brought new hope. Quickly taking off her helmet, she took over at the lights. Using hand signals, she held up all the traffic heading into the town centre before allowing the cars of spectators to turn right. In no time at all she had everything moving.

The police woman smiled and gave a thumbs up as the mini bus turned right. From the back seat Marcus gave a great roar of delight, 'That's really cool. That's cool.'

Two stewards in orange jackets standing at the entrance to the main car park had obviously been told to look out for the mini bus. The larger, a gentle gum-chewing giant of a man, signalled for Alan to stop and strolled over to have a word. 'No need to go in there, guv,' he said. 'Just carry on to the far end and Jack'll let you into the players' car park.' He slapped the side of the mini bus to show that they should move on. 'Enjoy your game, lads and lasses.'

Alan bumped across the car park and parked alongside the Anniversary Lane mini bus. Glancing into the mirror, he watched Hardeep and Ms Granger bouncing up and down like super balls on strings as the sports car negotiated the loose mix of sand and old half broken bricks which would no doubt soon be covered by a coating of tarmac.

Ms Granger parked, smiled and waved to the waiting team. Looking a little unwell for a moment, Hardeep took some time to move. However, after fiddling with his seat belt, he eventually levered himself out of his seat.

'Just thought I'd like to come and cheer you along,' he boomed.

'Fine,' said Alan, 'but no shaking hands until after the game!'

A peak-capped doorman guided the team through a maze of corridors underneath the main stand. Soon they found themselves in the club's new trophy room. Here Jed was waiting for them, leaning casually against a display cabinet full of reminders of the long-off glory days in the early 1960's when Bridley F.C. had been one of the best teams in the land.

Offering words of welcome, Jed promised that everyone would see the whole Bridley v Banchester match from seats specially reserved in the family enclosure. 'Just you make sure you've got your boots on ready for your half time slot,' he warned. Heads nodded in eager agreement until a loud roar from overhead signalled that Bridley players were leaving the pitch after completing their warm up. 'You'll have to hurry to take your seats now. Keep your eyes open and watch how professionals spread out and use the whole pitch. And watch out for Gary Ramsbottom.

He used to be a good 'un but he won't get a kick today!' joked Jed.

Dale and Carl, two players from Bridley's youth team, were to be the school's hosts for the day. With their hair closely cropped and somewhat ill at ease in smart grey suits, they seemed reluctant at first. But they cheered up remarkably quickly when Charmaine asked for their autographs. 'Might be famous players one day and anyway I need them for my big sister,' she tried to explain. The Lewis twins, who knew she hadn't got any sisters, were far from convinced.

The players guided the Hoddle Street team down a flight of stairs until they emerged in a tunnel which again appeared to be under the main stand. Here Anniversary Lane were already waiting. Obviously also determined to make the most of their big day out, each team member was wearing a new track suit with the letters ALP printed on the front. 'Just thought you'd like to catch the real atmosphere before you take your seats,' said Carl, grinning. 'And just think, in about five minutes' time Banchester United players will be standing where you are now!' added Dale.

'I know we're ancient rivals, but you're not thinking of playing are you?' joked Alan as he shook hands with Eric Murray, the track-suited Headteacher from Anniversary Lane. 'Might make a guest appearance if we find ourselves a couple of goals down,' responded Eric, laughing.

For a moment conversation ceased as both coaches seemed to have a lot on their minds. Games between the schools had always been played in a friendly and sporting way. But what would happen today? Would anyone let themselves down? Would anybody prove to be a poor loser? Both men seemed worried that one or two children might not be able to handle the occasion. 'I hope their nerves don't get to them,' said Eric.

'Man, this is going to be great,' murmured Marcus, turning confidently to Balraj and Bernard who were standing next in line. 'The crowd sound very loud,' said Balraj, a little nervously. 'What's that?' groaned Bernard longingly as the stomach-tempting smell of burgers and onions drifted in through the tunnel entrance. 'I think we'd better get these lads and lasses to their seats or they'll all be wanting food,' said Alan with a smile.

The smell of onions gave way to the scent of freshly mown grass as the teams moved along the touch line to the family enclosure. Somewhat disappointed, they made their way unnoticed, for most eyes appeared to be fixed on a troupe of dancers in the centre circle. ' I bet they're going to be a lot more excited when Bridley and Banchester come through that tunnel!' said Charmaine, turning to speak to the Lewis twins.

But the announcer appeared to be less than happy with this quiet arrival. The tape accompanying the dancers was suddenly turned off. The sound of much magnified coughing echoed around the ground as he cleared his throat before speaking. Apparently a little uncertain whether he could be heard, he bellowed into the speaker. Even passing aliens aboard a space craft way out beyond Jupiter or Mars would have heard him: *'Let's have a special round of applause for children from Hoddle Street Juniors and Anniversary Lane Primary. For years they have been the best teams in the Bridley Year 6 league. At half time they will play a short match for our entertainment.'*

Polite applause broke out around the ground and the top of Alan Ramsbottom's head turned the colour of a Bridley Town football shirt. Balraj puffed out his chest like a budgie in a pet shop. At the same time Bernard's socks slipped to his ankles revealing spindly legs protected by borrowed shin pads. Soon everyone had settled, ready to join in the great roar of approval as the Bridley and Banchester players took to the pitch.

What can be said about the Bridley v Banchester match which is not already known? No doubt many readers saw the game live on Channel 6023. For those who missed the game, here is part of the match report in the Larkshire Saturday Pink. Reliable as ever, the paper was already hitting the counters of newsagents in Bridley by 6pm.

Bridley Town v Banchester United
This was not a game for the faint hearted. Those who doubt that professional players try their best in 'friendlies' should have been there to watch what turned out to be a cracker.

Bridley fans were thrilled to see Gary Ramsbottom in the Banchester line-up. A great cry of 'Gary is back. Gary is back' echoed around the ground as he took to the pitch for his first game 'back home' since his recent £5,000,000 transfer.

Even with three players away on international duty, Banchester could boast a star studded line-up. But that didn't stop the 'The Cloggers' from having a real go. Long balls, thumped in from the wings, upset the rhythm of Banchester players more used to close passing movements on their own bowling green of a pitch. Leading 3 – 0, Bridley left the pitch at half time to a standing ovation!

The second half was a different story. Much to the amazement of the Bridley crowd, Benito Scarletti came off the bench and in record quick time the world's most expensive striker had slotted home three goals.

With the score locked at 3-all and with Benito curling in shots from just outside the box, there seemed no chance that Bridley could hang on. But Chopper Simms, Bridley's silver-haired, knobbly-kneed pensioner of a full back, had not read the script. In the dying seconds of the game, he forced his aching limbs forward to support one last counter attack. In haste a Banchester defender headed the ball away from danger. The ball landed kindly in front of the Chopper's trusty left boot. Without hesitation, and with one almighty swing, he thrashed the ball into the roof of the net......
4 – 3!

It is only on these pages that the true story of what happened in the titanic struggle between Hoddle Street Juniors and Anniversary Lane Primary is told. For the report in the Saturday Pink was less than ten lines long and missed all the key details; and Channel 6023 showed advertisements throughout half time. Luckily many in the crowd caught the mood of the day. Large sections of the crowd clapped and cheered as the teams stepped nervously onto the turf.

But then Fred Smith, a highly experienced referee from the local Sunday morning league, looked extremely puzzled. The small goalposts and markers needed for the junior game were missing.

THE BIG MATCH

Fred had to act quickly. Result? The match was played on the full sized pitch! It is true this had its funny side. Under normal circumstances, Johnny Harvey, the excellent Anniversary Lane keeper, looked huge. But he seemed tiny once he had gone to stand in the goals down at the Brick Works end of the ground

Yet there was no danger that either keeper would need to make a save. For the pitch was far too big and nobody could get close enough to goal to take a shot. And in the excitement of the big match atmosphere players on both sides forgot to play their usual passing game. Instead, like packs of tiring hounds chasing a fox, the players struggled after the ball. By half-time the crowd was losing interest.

In all honesty it was hard to tell whether the Hoddle Street players heard anything of Alan Ramsbottom's team talk during the thirty seconds allowed to change ends. But there was no doubting that they heard the advice offered by Hardeep Singh from the front row of the family enclosure. 'PASS THE BALL AND MOVE INTO SPACE,' roared Hardeep so loudly that even the seats in the main stand began to shake.

It was then that Alan made a brave and unexpected tactical move. He took off both strikers, leaving everyone dumbfounded. For a moment Charmaine Bradley looked upset, but then she took the decision in typically good heart. In contrast, little Rob Tomkinson started to sulk.

The change allowed Hoddle Street's untried substitutes to make their mark. Chest puffed out and grinning from ear to ear, Balraj rushed onto the field eager to try his very best. Bernard, socks already slipping, followed a second or two later. Once on the field Bernard was an absolute revelation. With the determined look of a seasoned professional, he stormed forward. With a series of almost kangaroo-like hops, he suddenly found himself close to goal and cracked a shot which bounced off the cross bar and on into touch with the goalkeeper well beaten. Suddenly alive again, the crowd roared approval.

Balraj had far more natural skill but seemed to tired quite quickly. The little fleet-footed striker was still getting used to the size of the pitch when the referee blew his whistle for full time.

The 0-0 score delighted the crowd for it meant there would have to be a penalty shoot out. Spectators who had slipped out for a quick half time cup of tea now gripped the edge of their seats. A great roar echoed around the ground as the first Anniversary Lane player prepared to take the first kick.

All the early penalty takers were unlucky, for at first Fred Smith placed the ball on the spot intended for the Bridley v Banchester clash. The result was disappointing but predictable: ten consecutive kicks failed even to reach the keeper. Yet, with the crowd now really interested, the game could not be allowed to end on such an anti-climax.

Fortunately, the ref knew exactly what to do. For each remaining kick he placed the ball two steps closer to the goals. And then, keen to keep up the excitement, he encouraged the remaining penalty takers to run at full pace from the centre circle. Their surges downfield attracted a huge roar of appreciation from the Holt End.

This made all the difference. Anniversary Lane players now scored easily and Hoddle Street replied in kind. Coming back off the bench, Charmaine Bradley struck a cracker into the roof of the net. Bernard showed equal determination, striking the ball cleanly past Johnny Harvey's telescopic arm to make the score 4 – 4!

Finally it was down to just two penalty takers. In the centre circle the stocky centre back from Anniversary Lane looked scornfully at Balraj. 'Stick to cricket, sonny, and just watch me,' he boasted before gliding off towards the goal.

Up to this point Marcus had fully lived up to his father's opinion that he would never make a goalkeeper. His only contact with the ball had been when handing it to Fred Smith after each successful penalty.

Did Marcus sense that Anniversary Lane had a rotten apple? For suddenly things changed. As the Anniversary player moved to strike the ball, Marcus showed unexpected concentration. Then, at the last possible moment, he arched his body and dived wide towards the left. His guess, if guess it was, was inspired, for with arms fully outstretched he reached the ball and tipped it over the bar. A huge cheer went up in the Holt End behind the goal, whilst over in the family enclosure seats started to rattle as Hardeep Singh began to boom out support for his cousin: *'COME ON NOW, BALRAJ'*.

The goalkeepers touched hands and changed places. Every eye was now fixed on Balraj Singh who stood alone in the centre circle. Deep in concentration, an age seemed to pass before he made any move. Suddenly, as if awakened by the wave of support from around the ground, he took off. Almost too tired to keep up his pace, he appeared to hesitate part way towards the goal. But another surge of support from all around the ground pushed him onward.

'Come on Balraj,' shouted his team mates.

'You can do it,' shouted Alan.

'Keep going, you'll score,' roared Mrs Witherspoon.

'Keep looking up,' yelled Ms Granger.

'COME ON, BALRAJ. YOU CAN DO IT,' roared Hardeep.

Lifting his head, Balraj adjusted his stride and feinted to the left. Somehow he delayed his shot until Johnny Harvey dived. Then, like a golfer close to a green, he chipped the ball into the net.

Victory can sometimes be very sweet indeed!

A charter of rights

Every child has the right:

Not to have to fight

To expect people to be kind

Not to be made fun of

Not to be made sad

Not to be scared of the teachers

To have friends

Not to be scared to come to school

To be safe

Drafted by Year 3 children at a school in Manchester,
Quoted in Equality Assurance in Schools, Runnymede Trust, 1993

We are grateful to the Runnymede Trust for permission to reproduce this Charter.

Runnymede Trust (1993) Equality Assurance in Schools – Quality, Identity, Society: A handbook for Action, Planning and School Effectiveness, Stoke-on-Trent: Trentham Books with the Runnymede Trust, p. 14. [Available from Central Books, 99 Wallis Road, London E9 5LN]

No Footballs in the Playground can be ordered directly by writing to:

Leyburn Clovelly
PO Box 94
Houghton le Spring
Tyne and Wear
DH5 8JX

Payment can be either cheque or postal order made payable to Leyburn Clovelly. Please add the following to cover the cost of posting: £1.00 for the first book and 50p for each additional book to a maximum of £3.50.